Eileen Boggess

The Mia
Fullerton
Series

Eileen Boggess

bancroft
press

Published by Bancroft Press ("Books that enlighten")
P.O. Box 65360, Baltimore, MD 21209
800-637-7377
410-764-1967 (fax)
www.bancroftpress.com

Cover and interior design: Tammy Sneath Grimes, Crescent Communications
www.tsgcrescent.com • 814.941.7447

Author photo: Earl Hulst

Hardcover:
ISBN 1-890862-46-0
LCCN 2006922102

Paperback:
ISBN 1-890862-47-9
LCCN 2006936544

Printed in the United States of America

First Edition

3 5 7 9 10 8 6 4 2

For Todd, Erin, and Nolan
And my former seventh grade class at St. Pius X School

Chapter
One

Strapped into the front car of a giant roller coaster, I struggled against the shoulder harness, but couldn't escape its intense grip. An ominous *click, click, click* echoed in my ears as I was pulled to the summit of a monstrous hill. The car teetered precariously at the top, and my body tensed, waiting for the big drop.

At a deafening speed, I plunged downward, timidly peering over the top of my runaway car. With a white-knuckled grip on the safety bar, I screamed in horror. Past the first gargantuan hill, I was catapulted through the atmosphere, and crashed back to Earth looking like a meteor with a pony tail. Right before I became fertilizer, a thunderous voice exploded in my ears.

"Mia, it's high time you get up! Are you going to sleep your entire life away?"

Bolting upright in bed, twisted in a tangle of sheets, I came face to face with my mother. Catching my breath, I muttered, "I'm up already. Jeez, it's still summer break, in case you've forgotten."

"I've hardly forgotten, because you remind me of it every day," my mother said. "But my vacation is over, so I need you to get moving so I can get to work."

I raised my eyebrows. "You're not really going to wear that, are you?"

"What's wrong with this outfit?" My mom's red hair floated around her head in a halo of unmanageable curls as she looked down at her "flower power" T-shirt and bell-bottom jeans. "You used to like the way I dressed."

"I also used to like Pokémon, so I don't think what I *used* to like counts for much. Sometimes, a person needs to grow up."

"I refuse to change just because you don't approve of my funky clothes. Some people are happy with who they are and aren't constantly trying to change themselves."

"First of all, nobody says 'funky' any more, and secondly, forty-year-old women shouldn't wear tight T-shirts and hip hugging jeans."

"Excuse me, but I am only thirty-eight years old, and I can use any words I want because I am an English teacher, and etymology is my specialty."

"Isn't etymology the study of bugs?"

"No, etymology is the study of words. You'd better know things like that if you're going to be on the Academic Quiz Bowl team this year."

I rolled my eyes as my mom droned on.

"I'll be in my classroom, and Dad's at the office, if you need to reach either of us. And remember to wear your retainer and make sure you and Chris eat a healthy lunch—not what you ate yesterday."

"What's wrong with fish and chips?"

"Goldfish crackers and corn curls do not qualify as a nutritious meal."

"Fine, I'll feed the dork some granola."

"Look, as the older sister, you're expected to lead by example." She kissed me on the top of my head. "And I don't want you two watching TV all day."

"What would we watch? We don't have cable. You know, even people in prison have cable, Mom."

"Maybe that's why they're in prison in the first place—they watched too much TV when they were young." She headed toward the door and I dropped the TV issue. I had a much bigger battle to fight today. Tilting my head to the side, I put on my most innocent expression.

"What do you think about teaching seniors next year? They need a good teacher to get them ready for college term papers, and I know how much you get into writing thesis statements."

She ran her fingers through her hair.

"How many times have we had this conversation? I'm the freshman English teacher at St. Hilary's High School, and you're stuck with me this coming year. You should be glad someone who loves you will be grading your essays."

"If you really loved me, you wouldn't torture me by being my teacher. Most of my friends hardly ever see their parents, but I'm being forced to spend more time with you. I'm being given a prison sentence—without cable TV, I might add—of having to see you every day for over an hour."

"There are worse things in life than spending time with your mom."

I sighed. "If you're so intent on ruining my life, can you at least promise me you won't dress up like Sherlock Holmes when you do the Sir Arthur Conan Doyle unit? And that you won't wear the wizard's cloak for your unit on fantasy literature? You look like a freak."

"I like my costumes, and so do my students."

"Your students think you're weird, Mom."

"I may be weird, but I'm also going to be your teacher next year." She continued toward the door. "Oh, by the way, a new family is finally moving into the Petersons' house next door. Why don't you bake some cookies and take them over as a house warming present? Maybe they'll have some kids your age to play with."

"Mom, I'm fourteen, not seven—I don't *play* any more. And there's no way I'm going over to a stranger's house with cookies."

"Why? It'll make them feel welcome and it'll give you something to do."

"I wouldn't even know what to say to them."

"You'd say, 'Here are some cookies, and welcome to the neighborhood.' It amazes me how you can shoot your mouth off to your family with absolutely no trouble at all, yet you're too terrified to utter a peep to a stranger." She looked at her watch. "Look, I know you get nervous talking to new people, but I need your help. And I'm really late, so I've got to get going." She hurried from my room, leaving behind a trail of Birkenstock shoeprints.

After I heard the front door slam, I reached under my bed and pulled out my library book: *Excruciatingly Shy: How to Defeat Public Fear and Become Popular.* "Chapter One: Methods for Mastering Social Anxiety: Face Your Fears and Commit to Change." I snuggled into my pillows. Good-bye, "Mia the Meek."

"Exercise one: Imagine you are at a party and someone asks you to dance." I closed my eyes and imagined Jake in my arms.

"Are you having a seizure or something?" I opened my eyes and saw Chris, his red, curly hair matted from sleep.

I turned my attention back to my book. "Get out of my room."

Chris scratched his stomach, pulled up his oversized boxer shorts, and burped. "What are you reading, *The Joys of Geekdom?*"

I covered the title with my hand, but he pulled the book away from me and laughed.

"*Excruciatingly Shy: How to Defeat Public Fear and Become Popular?* You're a bigger loser than I thought. Jake Harris will never like you, no matter what you read."

"What do you know about Jake Harris? Have you been reading my diary again?"

"Only when I need help falling asleep." Chris tossed the book on the foot of my bed. "Reading a book isn't going to stop people from calling you 'Mia the Geek.'"

"The name is Mia the *Meek,* and for your information, I'm no longer going to be known by that name. This year, I'll be known as 'Mia the Magnificent.'"

"More like Mia the Moron," Chris replied.

"If your brain was chocolate, it wouldn't fill an M&M," I said, picking up my book.

"Come on, tell me how you're going to try to become normal—I could use a good laugh."

"All right, I'll tell you, but only since you're begging me to." I put my book down and laid out my plan. "You see, I figured out there were two classes per grade at Assumption, and each one had about twenty-five students in it."

"And how long did it take you to figure that out?"

"Oh, shut up," I said. "Do you want to hear my plan or not?" I pushed him away. "And what are you doing? Get away from me!"

"I was just listening to see if I could hear the ocean." He sat back on the end of my bed and started picking between his toes. "Well, don't stop there, Einstein. I can't wait to be blown away by the rest of this amazing scheme."

"Have you ever considered suing your brain for non-support?" I took a deep breath, praying for patience *and* the restraint not to kill him. "Anyway, me and my classmates have all gone to school together at Assumption since kindergarten, so I've been with the same 49 people for approximately 1,620 school days."

"So?"

"So, I know every disgusting detail of their lives, and vice versa. But I start high school at St. Hilary's next week and a lot of people there won't have heard of Mia the Meek. I'm changing myself into a new, more outgoing me."

"Will the new you be as ugly as the old you?"

"Sometimes I wonder what you'd be like if you'd had enough oxygen at birth."

"All right, keep talking about this miraculous makeover. I'll yawn when I'm interested."

"That's it," I said, holding out my hands, palms up. "That's my whole plan."

"That's it? By reading a dumb book, you think you'll be able to change yourself into some big party girl? You are so bent. Don't you know that popular kids have either got it or they don't? And you definitely don't have it."

"I should've known better than to try talking to you like a human being rather than a primate." I pointed to the door. "And if you don't leave my room this instant, I'll tell Mom you have a *Victoria's Secret* catalog under your bed."

"Then I'll show Mom your diary with all your fantasies about Jakey-poo."

I got out of bed and stood an inch from his face. "I'll give you one last warning: Get out of my room, or else."

"Only if you promise you'll miss me," Chris replied, running out the door and slamming it behind him.

Faced with another monotonous morning stuck with the ignoramus imbecile, I lay back on my bed and stared out the window. The movers were hauling in our new neighbors' furniture. It all looked boring and beige. So as not to prolong the misery of being forced to hand cookies over to strangers, I wearily hoisted myself out of bed and headed down to the kitchen to whip up my special recipe of chocolate chip cookies. If I timed it right, the neighbors would be so busy with the movers that I could drop the cookies and run.

Chapter
Two

I'd just placed the last of the cookies on the counter to cool when I heard the roar of a motor and the grinding of gears. Looking out the window, I saw the moving truck thundering out of sight.

"Oh no, I'm too late."

"Too late for what?" Chris asked, walking into the kitchen and shoving a cookie into his mouth. I threw a bunch of cookies on a plate and handed it to him.

"Mom wants you to take these over to the new neighbors'."

"Get real. I heard Mom and you talking this morning. She told you to take them over."

"I'll give you five dollars."

"And miss watching you hyperventilate talking to a *spooky stranger?*"

"Your whole purpose in life is to serve as a warning to others." I grabbed the plate of cookies from Chris and stormed out the back door, with him following doggedly at my heels. While I still had the nerve, I marched up to the neighbors' front porch and forced myself to ring the doorbell. Instantly, a kid about my brother's age appeared, bouncing a soccer ball on his knee.

Before I could say anything, Chris asked, "Want to come over to my house and play soccer? I live right next door and I already have a goal set up."

"Cool." The kid turned around and yelled into his house: "Hey,

Mom, I'm going over to our neighbor's house. See you later!"

Before it fully registered, Chris and his new best friend disappeared. Panic swept over me at the prospect of being left alone on a stranger's stoop. I was just about to drop the cookies and run when a gorgeous guy with thick brown hair and the body of a Greek god appeared in the doorway, causing my legs to become utterly useless.

I locked eyes with him and realized they were the same shade of mocha brown as my favorite teddy bear, Mr. Snuggles. I immediately shifted my gaze, and that's when I saw he was holding the book *Whisper*. A cute guy with Mr. Snuggles's eyes reading my favorite book? This was too good to be true.

He asked through the screen door, "May I help you?"

I held out the plate. "Would you like some cookies?" *Oh God, I sound like a deranged Girl Scout!*

He opened the door a crack.

"Are you part of the welcome wagon or something?"

"Um, yes. I mean no. Uh, I mean . . ." I jabbed the plate of cookies into his gut. "Here." I turned and sprinted down the porch steps, wondering how hard it would be to convince my parents we had to move immediately.

"Wait a minute. What's your name?"

Not stopping, I called over my shoulder, "Mia."

"Mia, can you wait a second? I need your help."

I was a sucker for a gorgeous guy in need. I bit my lip and turned around.

"I need to find my brother, Kevin. He's about five and a half feet tall, brown hair, and extremely annoying. He's supposed to be helping me unpack the boxes for our bedrooms. Have you seen him?"

I nodded my head. The guy looked at me curiously.

"Can you tell me where he is?"

I took a deep breath. "He's at my house next door playing soccer with my little brother, Chris. Would you like me to get him for you?"

"No, I'll do it." From the plate, he grabbed a couple of cookies and shoved one into his mouth. "These are awesome."

"Thanks," I mumbled, making a beeline for my backyard. He set the cookie plate down on his porch and jogged beside me.

"Don't you want to know my name?"

I nodded, too petrified to speak.

"It's Tim. Tim Radford." I nodded again and he said, "You don't talk much, do you?"

I shrugged my shoulders. *Oh God, why did my backyard suddenly seem a million miles away?*

"Any chance you've read the book *Whisper*?"

I nodded.

"Cool! I just finished it and I'm dying to talk to someone about it. Didn't you think it was totally radical how the government took over people's lives by implanting brain chips?"

Before my brain could stop my mouth, I exclaimed, "And wasn't it cool how they figured out in the end how they should build relationships with people, not machines?"

He stopped walking.

"*Relationships*? You make it sound like a romance novel."

"I didn't mean relationships like that." Why did I open my mouth? I should have stuck to nodding. I wet my lips and continued, "I meant how all the people in the book have to talk to each other through machines and how that affects their feelings for each other."

"*Feelings*? It's about government control."

"I know there's government control in the book, but I think the most important idea is about human interaction."

"*Human interaction*? What are you, a thesaurus? I think you missed the big picture. You should read the book again."

"But I've already read it three times!"

"You had to read *Whisper* three times? I only need to read a book once to understand it."

We arrived in my backyard and I headed directly for my door. If talking to strangers was going to be this hard, staying shy wasn't all that bad an option.

Tim called to my retreating back, "If you need to read *Whisper* a fourth time, you can borrow my copy. I can even highlight all the important points, so you won't miss them this time."

I slammed the door behind me, remembering I never really liked Mr. Snuggles all that much anyway. I picked up the phone to call my best friend, Lisa, so I could give her the 4-1-1 on my new neighbor. After several rings, Lisa's mom, Mrs. Davis, answered. Mrs. Davis has a doctorate in psychology and I think she was secretly conducting a case study on me. Not wanting to give her any more research material, I quickly asked for Lisa.

"I'm sorry, Mia. Lisa is at her grandparents until school starts. They surprised us with a visit last night and took Lisa home with them. I have a theory they're using Lisa as an attachment figure to compensate for some sociological need they're missing in their lives. By the way, how are you feeling about starting high school next week?"

Not knowing if she meant physically or mentally, I replied, "I feel great, Mrs. Davis, but I have to go. I hear my brother calling for me," and hung up the phone.

I plopped down on a stool at the kitchen counter, thinking, *Next week, I'm going to conquer ninth grade, and then it's the world.* Figuring I would need a lot of energy to do all this conquering, I finished off the rest of the cookies on the counter.

Chapter
Three

My dad popped his head in my bedroom doorway. "How about a little one-on-one?" he asked.

I sucked up the last dust bunny from under my bed and switched off the vacuum cleaner.

"I'd do anything to get out of Mrs. Clean's evil empire. Look at the bruises I have on my knees from scrubbing baseboards all week."

"A little elbow grease never hurt anyone." My dad looked at me closely. "Aren't you supposed to be wearing your retainer?"

I sighed. "I'll get it and meet you outside." Positioning my retainer in my mouth, I combed my hair into a ponytail and joined him.

Once outside, my dad tossed me the ball.

"Ladies first."

I checked the ball to him to start the game and then immediately scored.

"Bet you're sorry you're such a gentleman."

Coming back with a long shot from the corner of the court, he said, "I'm not that much of a gentleman."

Within minutes, we were battling back and forth, point for point. With my dad breathing hard, I looked to take advantage by driving the lane for a lay-up over his head. The shot scored, but as I came down, I tripped and landed flat on my face, my chin bouncing off the pavement. My dad ran over to me.

"Are you all right?"

"Yeah, I think so," I said, rubbing my chin. "But my retainer flew out of my mouth. Do you see it?"

"It's over here."

We turned in unison to see Tim pointing at his shoe, my retainer perched on top of it. My dad whistled.

"Wow, what are the odds of that?"

Not in the mood for statistics, I grabbed my retainer off Tim's shoe and popped it back in my mouth. When it occurred to me where it had been, I gagged, spitting it back into my hand.

"Sorry about interrupting your game," Tim said, "but I came over to ask if you know of a good pizza place around here. My mom's tired of unpacking and wants to go out to eat tonight."

I stood mute, mesmerized by the remnants of my saliva dripping down his shoe.

"For the best pizza, you should try Nick's on the corner of Vine and Birch Street," my dad replied. "And thanks for cushioning the blow of Mia's retainer. She's got to wear that every day for the next year."

"No problem." Tim glanced at me. "You know, if you'd used your left foot to push off of for your lay-up, you would've had more control on your landing and might not have fallen on your face. I guess your basketball skills are about equal to your reading ability."

My jaw dropped at the insult and I tried to figure out a quick and clever comeback. Because nothing came to me, retreat seemed like the best defense. I stomped off to my house and slammed the back door as hard as I could. Walking past the hallway mirror, I caught a brief glimpse of myself: sweaty, greasy hair; dirt streaked down my face, an oozing scrape on my chin; and a filthy retainer in my hand. I was a vision of loveliness. Things couldn't get any worse.

Then I remembered: school started the next morning.

My roller coaster car was inches from slamming into the ground when I awoke, panting profusely. Switching off my alarm clock, I flopped back down on my stomach and closed my eyes.

"Mia, it's time to get up! Are you going to sleep your entire life away?"

Rolling my eyes under my closed eyelids, I crawled out of bed. After a long, hot shower, I slowly rejoined the land of the living. I buttoned my mandatory white blouse and tucked it into my uniform skirt—green and blue plaid—that all freshmen and sophomore girls were forced to wear at St. Hilary's. Looking in the mirror, I sighed with defeat. Unless polyester Scottish wear suddenly hit the catwalk in Paris, I was doomed to remain a fashion *don't*.

Turning my back to my reflection, I raced down the stairs and grabbed my backpack and a granola bar from the kitchen counter. Trying to avoid the standard, first-day-of-school picture in our front yard, I yelled, "I'm leaving," and ran out the back door. Checking to make sure my dad wasn't following me with a telephoto lens, I opened my granola bar and headed to Lisa's house. She lived up the street from me, and I think the main reason we first became friends was out of convenience. Proximity was everything then because my parents wouldn't let me cross the street alone.

Lisa emerged from her front door looking blonde, petite, and perky—as usual. As I watched her four-foot-ten-inch frame bounce down the stairs, I suddenly felt like the Jolly Green Giant, except I'm not very jolly—or green.

She smiled.

"So, are you ready for your big transformation?"

"I don't know," I said after a brief hesitation. "Now that the first day of school is here, I don't think I'm ready to go through with it. Just look at me."

"You look fine."

"Maybe it's better if I don't go through with it. I mean, high school is a big enough transition as it is. I shouldn't try to change too much at once."

"Too late. You already got rid of the glasses and braces. Now it's time to get rid of Mia the Meek."

"But what if people don't like the new me?"

"There's way too much to accomplish in life to spend time worrying about what other people think. When is some of my confidence going to rub off on you?"

"You have every right to be confident. You're one of the smartest teenagers in America. I mean, who else in the world organizes their iPods to make their brains bigger?"

"Not bigger, just more efficient. I told you: I read a study that if you alternate listening to different rhythm patterns in music, you can increase the synapses between your neurons, thereby increasing your brain capacity. For example, the number of synapses for a typical neuron is somewhere between one and ten thousand, but I plan to double the synapses in my neurons, so I can learn even more in the future."

"Uh-huh."

Lisa sighed.

"All right, I can see I lost you. Anyhow, if you weren't smart, you wouldn't have made St. Hilary's Freshman Academic Quiz Bowl team."

I chewed on a hangnail.

"I'm convinced Mr. Harrison made a mistake when he corrected our tests last year."

Lisa pulled my hand from my mouth.

"Stop that. You know he didn't make a mistake. I ran into Ms. Jackson, the high school TAG teacher this summer, and she said after reviewing our files, she thinks we have a chance to win! So, I spent all summer studying and can easily handle all the science questions. Jason Blevins, that guy from Sacred Heart, is our math guy. Mike Finnegan is freakishly smart in social studies. And you're an excellent literary source. We're going to crush the other teams."

"I don't think my personality allows me to do much crushing."

"We're starting high school, made the Quiz Bowl team, and are going to be on student council." She put her tiny hands on her tiny waist. "What could possibly go wrong?"

"Math. Mr. Grizzling hates me. Ever since I was a little kid and accidentally spilled coffee on his lap when I was visiting my mom, he's been out to get me."

"You're paranoid. Mr. Grizzling isn't going to fail you if you do the work," Lisa said impatiently. "What else have you got?"

"Well, what about the fact I will be fifteen in two months and I've never even come close to kissing a guy? It would be a fate worse than death if I actually lived the phrase 'sweet sixteen and never been kissed.'"

"You could kiss Mike Finnegan any time you want."

"Yeah right," I sighed. "You know Mike has the 'Nice Guy But' syndrome. He's a nice guy, but—"

"Personally, I think Mike's got a nice butt, and if he liked me, I'd be thrilled."

"You can have him," I said, slowing my pace. "I think I need to go back home—I don't feel so well."

Lisa grabbed my arm and dragged me down the sidewalk.

"No you don't. You spent all summer preparing to get rid of Mia the Meek, and today's the day we bury her for good!"

Chapter
Four

A sea of voices and slamming locker doors greeted us in the freshman hallway of St. Hilary's Catholic High School. I'd been down this hallway a million times before on my way to see my mom, but today was different. I wasn't a visitor—I was a student. I was like a foreigner who'd traded in her passport for a green card. I just hoped the natives were friendly and I could fake my way into their culture.

Finally making it to my locker, I looked across the hallway and whispered to Lisa, "I can't believe it. There are over two hundred people in our freshman class, and we get stuck with lockers across the hall from Stephanie Rasco, Jessie Carson, and Cassie Foster?"

Lisa immediately turned to look.

"Stop it," I said. "They'll see you."

"Who cares?" Lisa asked, turning her attention back to her combination.

"I care. I don't want Cassie to notice me. Remember what she did to Maggie?" My mind flashed back to kindergarten. My friend, Maggie Fletcher, used to be crazy in love with horses. Her folders were covered in horse stickers, her favorite movie was *National Velvet*, and every day she wore her hair tied back in a scrunchie so it would hang down her back like a horse's tail. All the girls fought to play with Maggie's hair during story time and, even at the age of five, Cassie couldn't stand anyone getting more attention than her.

One day, Cassie confiscated a pair of scissors from the scissor box, and lured Maggie behind the dumpster by telling her she had a new horse poster to give her. Once they were out of sight from the teacher on duty, Cassie hacked off Maggie's ponytail. After recess, Maggie was found crying, huddled in a ball behind the dumpster, clutching her severed ponytail in her hand. Every student was called into the office, one by one, and asked what they had seen. No one said anything and Maggie kept her silence. Not long after, Maggie lost her fascination with horses. And ever since that day, I've kept my distance from Cassie.

Opening her locker, Lisa replied, "Maggie got her ponytail chopped off a long time ago. And don't worry about those three. They'll peak in high school and then spend the rest of their lives reliving their glory days. In fact, by the time they're thirty-five, I bet they'll have more plastic in them than a recycling center."

When Cassie glanced over at us, I averted my eyes, hoping that if I didn't see her, she wouldn't see me. Unfortunately, that trick hadn't worked when I was three, and it wasn't working now, either.

Striding over to me on legs I swear went up to her chest, Cassie asked, "What's that big, red, crusty mark on your chin, Mia the Meek?"

"'Hi to you too," Lisa replied, staring into Cassie's icy blue eyes without flinching.

"I—I fell down playing basketball," I stammered.

"You know, they have make-up for that sort of thing." Cassie ran her fingers through her newly cropped, white-blonde hair.

"My parents won't let me wear make-up," I said. *Now why did I give her that ammunition against me?*

"Oh, I'm sorry. Make-up could *really* help your looks."

"Yeah, but no matter what Mia the Meek does to herself, she's still so ugly she'd make blind kids cry," Stephanie said. Her red, curly hair bounced around her shoulders and her green eyes sparkled. Stephanie was never happier than when she was dissing someone.

Cassie crossed her arms across her ample chest.

"And why are you blinking so much? Did you develop a tic over the summer?"

"I got contacts," I said, looking away self-consciously. "They're sort of new, so sometimes I have to blink to get my eyes used to them."

"At least they're better than your glasses. They were the worst. And I'm glad you grew your hair out," Jessie said, flipping her own perfectly smooth chestnut brown hair over her shoulders. I'd never seen anyone who could flip her hair as perfectly as Jessie. She must've spent hours practicing.

"Whatever," Cassie said. "I just came over to tell you I saw your mom this morning, and whatever kind of look she was going for, she missed." Cassie laughed as she and her evil compatriots turned and walked away, their butts swaying in perfect unison.

I watched them walk into Mr. Benson's American History classroom and groaned.

"They're all in my first period class this year? What did I do to deserve this?"

"If we have first period together, we probably have the same class schedule. It looks like we'll have to put up with the Easy Bake Oven cakes for the year," Lisa replied.

"'Easy Bake Oven cakes'?"

"Think about it: The cakes that come with an Easy Bake Oven look cute and sweet on the box cover, but once you bake them, you realize they're small, nasty, and not worth the time," Lisa explained as we walked into the room.

"Lisa, Mia, over here," Maggie called, waving us over to a group of desks. "We saved you some seats."

We climbed into the seats behind Maggie and her best friend, Kelly Martin.

"Did you guys have a good summer?" Maggie asked as we got settled.

"The best," Lisa said. "I got to go to a camp for junior MENSA members."

"MENSA?" Kelly asked.

"It's for people who score in the top two percent on a standard-ized IQ test," Lisa explained. "I took an IQ test just for fun at my mom's office, and I scored so high, my mom enrolled me in this camp."

"You took an IQ test just for fun?" Maggie asked.

"Your IQ is in the top two percent?" Kelly added.

"The camp was awesome. We spent the week working on logic, philosophy, math, science, and a little bit of Latin."

"And to think, I was proud of myself for reading a book this sum-mer," Kelly remarked.

I grabbed Lisa's arm.

"There truly *is* a God. Jake Harris's sitting right over there!"

Lisa turned to look.

"Are you ever going to get over your obsession with him?"

"Or do something about it?" Kelly said.

"Don't you remember when I joined the track team in middle school?" I asked, bringing up my short-lived attempt at organized sports.

"You only joined because I made you," Maggie said.

"True." But secretly, I wanted to fulfill at least one of my fantasies involving Jake. My running fantasy consisted of winning a city-wide track meet while looking fabulous, my hair flowing behind me like a shampoo commercial. Jake would be on the sidelines, cheering me on as I crossed the finish line way ahead of my competition. At the end of the race, he'd sweep me up in his arms as the entire city broke into thunderous applause.

So, I joined the track team. But after the first practice, I came to the realization that running sucked. I probably would've given up that very day if Maggie hadn't urged me to keep going—and I hadn't seen how great Jake's legs looked in shorts. Fortunately, as the sea-son progressed, every practice got a little easier and Jake got better looking, so all of my pain seemed worth it—until the afternoon my running fantasy with Jake came to a screeching halt.

It had been a particularly grueling practice, and I was doing my usual cool-down routine of walking around the playground with my hands on my hips, trying to catch my breath. Runners, I'd discovered, are fond of spitting, and I was secretly proud of how good I'd become at spewing spit. I'd just hurled a particularly impressive lugey across the grass when Jake walked by and said, "Nice shot, dude!"

I freaked out. The future father of my children had just seen me hawk a lugey! Not knowing what to say or do, I panicked and sprinted inside the school. Then I hid in a bathroom stall until I was sure everyone had left.

My track team career ended that afternoon. But surprisingly, I developed a passion for running, which I continue to do on my own—of course, only in places where no one can see me hawking post-run lugeys.

I sighed, gazing across the room at Jake.

"Just look how gorgeous he is. I mean, he's perfect: blonde hair, a body to die for, a great smile, and green eyes with tiny specks of gray in them."

"How do you know his eyes have specks of gray in them?"

"I studied his yearbook picture," I said.

Maggie interrupted. "Did you hear that Jake and Cassie broke up?"

"No way! Where did you hear that?" I asked eagerly. "They've been going out for two years."

"Collin Dewhurst—that cute guy sitting next to Jake—told me last week at our first cross-country practice that Jake and Cassie had some sort of fight and broke up. I guess they're still friends and stuff, but Jake's available, Mia."

"Like I have a chance with him. The last words Jake spoke to me were back in seventh grade, when he complimented me on a lugey."

"At least it's a start," Maggie remarked.

"It's probably for the best," I said. "If Jake ever spoke to me, I'd simply die."

"If Jake spent as much time on his homework as he does searching the web for the latest slang, he might actually do well in school, or at least pass his classes," Lisa said as she organized her notebooks.

"When I look at Jake, I'm not thinking about his brain."

"Look, there's Mike." Lisa waved her arms over her head and yelled, "Mike, over here!"

After Mike slid into the desk next to mine, Lisa said, "Have you seen Jason Blevins yet? I wanted to talk to him about the Quiz Bowl."

"No, I heard Jason moved over the summer," Mike said. "He's not going to be on our Academic Quiz Bowl team after all."

"What?" Lisa cried. "Jason was supposed to be our math expert! What are we going to do?"

"I don't believe it," I said.

Lisa shook her head.

"I know it's terrible, Mia. I spent all summer studying scientific formulas, when I should have been working on math equations."

"Not that. I can't believe who just walked in the door."

Lisa strained her neck to look.

"Who's that guy?"

"Tim Radford, my new neighbor. He thinks he's God's gift to the world."

"Obviously, he isn't the only one who thinks so," Lisa remarked as Cassie grabbed hold of Tim's arm and led him to a seat near her own.

Mr. Benson stood up and asked Lisa and me to come up to his desk. "I just wanted to remind you about the informational meeting about student council today after school. Your mom mentioned you two might be interested in joining, and if you're seriously interested in contributing to what goes on at St. Hilary's, I'd be glad to have you on our team. We'll be nominating people for president and vice president of the freshman class, so it's very important you attend if you wish to have your voices heard."

"We'll be there, Mr. Benson," Lisa quickly replied, not giving me a chance to say no.

"Great. Now get back to your seats so I can start class."

We headed to the back of the room and I whispered, "Thanks a lot. I didn't want to go out for student council. I mean, why should we even hold an election? Cassie's going to be president. She knows everyone, and even if she doesn't know them, they know her. She's already got this election wrapped up."

Lisa whispered, "Don't worry, I have a plan."

"What plan?"

"Girls, hurry up. I need to get started," Mr. Benson warned. I quickly climbed into my seat and scrunched down as he launched into a lengthy lecture on the struggles of our forefathers. Personally, I wished I'd had it as easy as they did; all they had to do was declare their independence, win a war of revolution, and write a constitution. I had to face my mother next period.

The bell rang starting second period, and my mom bellowed too loudly, "Welcome, literary giants! This will be the year when you'll dive into literature and let it become part of your lives. You'll discover a love of words hidden within you and astound me with your prose." Then she launched into a long, tedious lecture about assignments, books we'd read in class, and her expectations for the semester.

By the end of the period, most of my classmates were dying a slow death of boredom, but I was elated. Maybe my mom finally understood how much I hated being in her room. Maybe she wouldn't try to totally humiliate me this year. Maybe—

"I always end my first day by describing how literature can change your life." She beamed at me.

Then again, maybe not. My stomach lurched. I knew what was coming next: the *Petey and the Potty* story!

"My daughter, Mia, whom some of you already know—and if you don't—she's the pretty girl with brown hair sitting in the back of the room right now. Wave your arm so everyone knows who you are, Mia."

In a state of shock, I limply waved my hand.

"Anyway, Mia would simply not get potty trained. My husband and I thought she would wear diapers until she entered kindergarten. Then we got the book, *Petey and the Potty*. Mia loved that book! One day, she marched up to me and said, 'If Petey can go potty, I can too!' And she never wore diapers again after that.

"So, if Petey can change a small girl's life, imagine what great literature can do for you," my mom declared as the ending bell rang.

Gathering their books, my classmates thundered to the door as I sat immobilized in my chair. Lisa laughed.

"I've heard that story before, but every time your mom tells it, I crack up. I can just picture you sitting on your potty and reading that book. Hey, I wonder if she'll teach punctuation by telling everyone about your first menstrual period."

"Oh, shut up." I grabbed my books and stormed for the door. Stephanie was waiting for me in the hallway.

"Hey, Mia the Meek, my great-grandma has some diapers you can borrow if you need them."

I clenched my jaw and brushed past her, racing to my next class. I was going to kill my mom!

Tim ran after me. "Mia, wait up!"

I twirled around and looked him squarely in the eye.

"For your information," I said, "I've been going to the bathroom on my own for over ten years."

"Good for you. I was only going to let you know I picked up a pencil you dropped. But, because you brought the subject up, I understand now why you had so much trouble understanding *Whisper*. Potty training books must be more your style. If you want to borrow it, I think we still have a copy of *Willy Goes Wee Wee* from when my brother was a baby."

I glared at him.

"When I first met you, I didn't really like you. But now that I've gotten to know you better, I think I might hate you."

"At least your feelings are growing," Tim said as we walked into the science room together. Sister Donovan immediately grabbed both of our arms.

"Because you two are the last to arrive, you'll be lab partners. Now, go and take a seat across from Jake and Cassie."

"What? Sister Donovan," I pleaded, "I can't be partners with him!"

"Yes, you can and you will." She dragged us over to our table.

I reluctantly climbed onto my stool while Sister Donovan returned to the front of the room and began handing out worksheets on lab procedures. Cassie slid a note across the table to Tim and whispered, "If you have any questions about anything, here's my phone number. Call me."

Tim pocketed her number. "Thanks."

I rolled my eyes and turned away to catch Jake staring at me. Why was he looking at me like that? Oh my God! Did I have something hanging from my nose?

Jake smiled. "Dude, do I know you?"

I looked over my shoulder to see if he was talking to someone else, but when I turned back, he was still smiling at me.

"Jake, it's me, Mia Fullerton. We've gone to school together since kindergarten."

"No way, dude."

"It's Mia, you moron," Cassie said, rolling her eyes. "She got rid of her glasses and braces and grew out her hair."

Jake continued to check me out and I thought I had died and gone to heaven until Tim brought me crashing back to earth.

"Hey, speaking of braces, where's your retainer, Mia? Didn't your dad say you were supposed to wear it all the time?"

Without prying my eyes away from Jake's smile, I whispered at Tim out of the corner of my mouth, "Not now."

"Well, just make sure when you put it in, it stays in. I don't want it flying all over the room again."

Cassie wrinkled her nose in disgust. "Oh, gross! Mia's retainer flew out of her mouth?"

"It was the result of her flawed basketball skills."

"I sunk that shot!" I said, turning to face Tim. "I sacrificed my body for the points, and for your information, I'm an excellent basketball player. I bet I could wipe the court with you any day."

"That I would like to see," Tim said.

"You name the time and place and I'll be there."

"Tonight after dinner, I'll come over to your backyard. See, I'm a gentleman. I'm even giving you home court advantage."

"Fact is, it has to be on my basketball court. You don't have one at your house."

"So, I'm smart and a gentleman. I'll see you tonight."

"My pleasure."

"Whoa, Mia, you're like talking and stuff," Jake said. "Totally off the chain."

"So, what's the deal?" Tim persisted. "Are you going to put your retainer in or not? I need to know if I should take cover."

I reached into my backpack and jammed my retainer into my mouth.

"There! Are you satisfied? Now leave me alone."

"Certainly, especially because I know your retainer's a deadly weapon that you know how to use."

Chapter
Five

"I wonder who ever thought of taking a perfectly good fish and turning it into a tasteless stick," Lisa said, dousing her lunch in tartar sauce.

"It smells like Lent," I said, wrinkling my nose in disgust as I wrapped my retainer in a napkin and placed it on the edge of my tray.

Mike picked out a piece of brown banana swimming in his cherry Jell-O. "Well, we survived our first morning of high school. The only good thing that's happened to me so far is getting Lisa as my science lab partner."

Lisa beamed. "Thanks, Mike."

"And I got stuck with Tim Radford," I said as I opened my carton of chocolate milk and proceeded to spill it down the front of my white blouse. Dabbing at the stain with a napkin, I muttered, "I can't believe Tim thinks he's so much better than me."

"So, Mike, who will Ms. Jackson get to fill the fourth spot on the Academic Quiz Bowl team?" Lisa asked, ignoring me.

I scooped up some corn. "I mean, who does Tim think he is? There's no way he's smarter than me."

Mike shrugged. "I don't know—maybe Michelle McDonald, that really smart girl from St. Pius X."

"Tim even thinks he can beat me in basketball!"

Lisa shook her head.

"No, I heard Michelle isn't very good in math."

"I bet Tim can't even make a lay-up."

"Maybe there's someone from Holy Family. They have a pretty good math teacher."

"And then Tim had the nerve to remind me to wear my retainer!"

"The kids from Holy Family are too into sports."

I put my fork down. "Are either of you listening to me?"

"I heard every word," Lisa replied. "Tim is a jerk who obviously enjoys making you angry. Just try to ignore him, Mia."

"You're right. I won't talk about him again." I ate a spoonful of Jell-O. "But don't you think he's totally annoying?"

Lisa rolled her eyes at Mike.

"What? Oh, right. I'm not mentioning his name again." I picked up a fish stick and jabbed it into some tartar sauce. "But who is he to tell me I don't understand my favorite book?"

"You're spending a lot of energy on somebody you supposedly don't like," Lisa said, grabbing her tray and heading toward the garbage can.

I followed her and dumped in the remaining contents of my tray.

"I don't like Tim Radford. He's an idiot. Anyway, he's not even that cute. Jake is way cuter."

"Whatever. Just stop talking and grab your retainer so we aren't late for class."

I looked at my tray and then at the trash bin. Lisa followed my gaze.

"Don't tell me you just threw your retainer away."

I bit my lip, watching the garbage grow as student after student scraped their trays into the bin. "I just threw my retainer away."

"Well, you'd better hurry and get it. Your parents will kill you if you lose it."

"I am *not* digging through the garbage in front of the whole cafeteria. There are juniors and seniors in here."

"You have to. There's no other solution."

I tentatively reached my finger into the trash bin and flipped over a few napkins.

"I don't see it."

"Mia, you're going to have to reach into the garbage can to find it."

I gave Lisa a look of despair and slowly stuck my arms into the giant, gray rubber container, feeling my way through mounds of cherry Jell-O, lumpy tartar sauce, and soggy corn. Holding my breath, I picked through a heap of squishy fish and understood how Jonah must have felt.

"I'd like to stay with you and offer support," Lisa said, "but I promised Ms. Jackson I'd stop in before we see her this afternoon. Do you mind?"

"Go ahead. Why should we both smell like eau de trout for the rest of the day?"

"Thanks!" Lisa said, skipping out of the cafeteria while I moved aside so more students could dump their half-eaten food into the container.

After they walked away, I made one final plunge, digging to the middle of the heap. Thinking I saw my retainer, I leaned over the bin and probed deeper, when suddenly a wad of cherry Jell-O splashed into my hair.

"What?" Stephanie said. "I can't wait around all day while you go dumpster diving."

Tim, standing next to her, laughed. "What are you doing? Searching for Moby Dick?"

"Call me Ishmael," I growled as they walked away.

I was about to give up—or pass out from the stench—when finally I found my retainer perched on a hill of corn, still wrapped in the napkin. No garbage had touched it, so with a little disinfectant and a few hours of brushing, I might even be able to bring myself to wear it again.

Wiping kernels of corn off my arms, I muttered to myself and headed to the restroom.

I think I liked my life better when I was still Mia the Meek.

"Silence! I don't tolerate any noise in my classroom," Mr. Grizzling yelled as he handed out a sheet of paper to everyone. "The first item on my agenda for today's class is this list of rules. I expect them to be memorized, and there will be a test on each and every rule this Friday." He glared at us through his beady eyes. "Are there any questions?"

A kid I recognized from one of the mandatory religious retreats in middle school shouted without raising his hand, "Yeah, I've got a question. In rule number fifteen, what do you mean by asking us to keep our hands off 'other people's equipment'? That sounds kind of personal to me."

I began praying for the kid's life.

"Your name is Anthony Gellman. Is that correct?" Mr. Grizzling asked in a volume so low we had to strain to hear it.

"That's me," Anthony replied, ignoring the thick veil of tension covering the room.

"Well, Mr. Gellman, you have just earned yourself a week's worth of detention with me every day after school." Mr. Grizzling glowered. "Are there any further questions?"

We shook our heads mutely as Mr. Grizzling passed out a second round of papers.

"Good. Now get out a sharpened, number two pencil for a pretest on algebra. I expect all work to be shown. Anyone not showing work will have to redo the test after school."

I unenthusiastically picked up my pencil and began the test. As I struggled to figure out the purpose of combining perfectly harmless alphabet letters with tedious math problems, a horrific headache began brewing in my skull. Language and math should not be combined—it isn't natural. Glancing up to clear my head, I saw Tim completing his test with the vigor of Einstein. It figured he was a math guy—just one more reason for me to hate him.

During our study hall period, Ms. Jackson welcomed us to her room which, until last year, had been the janitor's closet.

"Good afternoon! How are we all surviving our first day of high school?"

Mike collapsed into a beanbag chair. "We just had Mr. Grizzling for math class. Can you believe it? He has twenty rules for his classroom!"

"All I care about is finding out who's going to fill the fourth spot on the Academic Quiz Bowl team," Lisa said.

As if on cue, Tim poked his head in the room. "Did you send for me?"

"Yes, I did," Ms. Jackson replied. "I'm Ms. Jackson, and this is Lisa Davis, Mike Finnegan, and Mia Fullerton."

"We've met." Tim smiled at me.

"I called for you because we would like you to join our team for the Academic Quiz Bowl. The Quiz Bowl is like a trivia contest, with questions from all the different academic areas, and some current events thrown in. During the tournament, we compete against other ninth grade teams from across the state, and it's our hope to bring the trophy back home to St. Hilary's."

"There is no hoping—we *will* bring the trophy home," Lisa interrupted determinedly.

Ms. Jackson continued, "The tournament is the first weekend in November, so we have only eight weeks to prepare. We'll meet daily during study hall, so you'll have to complete all your homework at home. Would you like to be part of our team?"

Tim grinned broadly. "If you want to win, then I'm your man."

"I love a guy with confidence!" Lisa exclaimed.

Mike pounded knuckles with Tim. "I'm glad I won't be outnumbered. We needed another guy on this team."

Ms. Jackson prodded me gently. "Mia, what do you have to say to our new team member?"

Overwhelmed by the odor of fish clinging to my clothes and the aroma of old disinfectant hanging in the air, I felt I was going to heave.

I tried to escape Ms. Jackson's room, but it was too late—I grabbed the trash bin and threw up.

As the rest of the team stood in horrified silence, Tim said, "A simple 'welcome to the team' would have been enough, Mia."

Chapter

I pleaded with the school nurse, Mrs. Olson. "See? I don't have a temperature and I feel perfectly fine. Can I go back to class now, please?"

"Are you sure you don't want to go home?" she asked doubtfully. "I don't want a flu epidemic hitting the school during the first week of classes."

"I have to go to the student council meeting after school today. I told Mr. Benson I'd be there."

"All right, as long as you promise me that if you feel sick again, you'll head straight to the restroom. Our custodian, Mr. Corrigan, has better things to do than clean up your vomit all day."

"I swear, the first sign of an upchuck, and I'm out of here." I crossed my heart. "By the way, is there any way you can call my dad and have him bring me a change of clothes and my toothbrush?"

"All right, settle down, guys," Mr. Benson said, calling the meeting to order. "First of all, I'd like to welcome all of you to your first year of student council at St. Hilary's. I'm the teacher representative for the ninth grade student council. This afternoon's meeting will focus on nominating class officers for next week's election. Has anyone thought about running for an officer position?"

Tuning him out, I looked around the room. A couple of guys

were playing paper football in the back while a group of girls next to me were doodling their boyfriends' names on pieces of paper. It all reminded me of last year's student council meetings. Somehow, I'd thought life would be different in high school. I'd thought I'd be surrounded by people who wanted to make a difference in the world—or at least in the school. Instead, I was stuck with a bunch of people who probably signed up for student council only because it would look good on their high school transcripts.

Suddenly, it occurred to me: Is this what life was going to be like—always expecting something better and more exciting, and then continuously being disappointed? What if nothing ever changed, and I lived out my life as a nobody? What if I was cursed with being shy the rest of my life? What if I never kissed anyone and died a lonely death? What if I threw up in school again?

A massive panic attack swept over me. I gasped, trying to catch my breath as sweat trickled down my face. Struggling to breathe, I realized I would flounder through the rest my life, uncertain of what to do or say in every situation presented to me. Instantly, there was no doubt in my mind that I'd remain a lumbering, reclusive loser who'd have to dig through trash bins for food.

Feeling utterly alone and completely immersed in the image of my future self wearing six layers of clothing and pushing a broken shopping cart down a dingy alley to my refrigerator box home, I suddenly heard my name being called from a great distance.

"Yes?" I croaked, swallowing what little spit there was left in my mouth.

"Great!" Mr. Benson beamed. "I'll need your campaign posters up by this Friday, and elections will be held on Monday of the following week. Good luck, and may the best person win!"

Students filed out of the room as I tried to figure out what had happened.

"What's Mr. Benson talking about?" I asked Lisa.

"What do you mean, 'What's Mr. Benson talking about?' You

were right there. After Jessie nominated Cassie for president of student council, I nominated you. Then, Jake Harris seconded my nomination, which really surprised me. Anyway, that was the plan I was telling you about earlier. I knew you wanted to make a big change in your life this year, so I thought I'd help by nominating you for ninth grade class president. I can't believe you actually went along with it. I mean, you didn't even hesitate when Mr. Benson asked you if you agreed to run. There may be hope for you yet."

"Are you crazy? There's no way I'm going to run against Cassie Foster for class president! That would mean people staring at me in the hallway, and I'd have to give a speech in front of over two hundred people!" I held my hands out for her to examine. "Look at my palms—they're breaking out in hives even thinking about it! I don't care what I said—I was in the middle of a delusion. I'm telling Mr. Benson to take back my nomination."

"No, you are not! Mia, this is going to be incredible. You are running against Cassie for class president, and I know you can beat her because I'll be your campaign manager." Lisa dragged me out of the classroom. "Now, let's get going—we have so much to do!"

"All I wanted was a simple, quiet year to work on my self-esteem. I don't think becoming the laughing stock of St. Hilary's is going to do much for my self-worth."

"But Jake Harris seconded your nomination! Doesn't that mean anything to you?"

"I don't care if Jake—" I stopped. "Are you telling me the truth about Jake?"

"Mia, you were right there. Didn't you notice Jake staring at you the whole meeting? That's why I thought you were getting all red and sweaty. Even Jake wants you for class president and not Cassie."

"Jake was really looking at me?" Chewing on my lip, I reluctantly said, "All right, I guess I'll run, but you have to promise me you won't get obsessed with this campaign. I'll hang a few posters and then give a gracious speech when I lose. Do you swear not to make too big a deal out of this, Lisa?"

I trudged up to my house and put my day in perspective—your typical combination of mortification, degradation, and humiliation. I couldn't wait to see what the next day would bring.

My mom opened the door and greeted me. "How are you feeling, honey?"

I glared at her.

"Don't 'honey' me. How could you possibly tell that *Petey and the Potty* story in front of my whole class? Don't you care about me at all?"

"I tell that story every year. It's so cute, and it playfully inspires students to read."

"Every year? Didn't you ever consider how much that story embarrasses me? You're always saying how you'll do anything for one of your students. Well, now that I'm forced into having you for a teacher, maybe you can care about me for a change!" I ran up the stairs to my room, slammed the door, and fell facedown on my bed.

A few minutes later, I heard a knock at the door.

"Mia, let me in."

I wiped away the tears that had been on the verge of falling all day and yelled, "The door's unlocked. You won't let me get a lock for it. Remember?"

My mom opened the door and sat down next to me on my bed.

"I'm sorry—this is new for me, too. From now on, I'll try not to tell any more of your secrets to the class. It's just that I know you have so much to offer others and you always hide your talents. Just once, I wish you would let others see how wonderful, smart, and loving you are." She ran her fingers through my tangled hair, which still had remnants of Jell-O in it. "I know I'm your mother, so of course I think you're brilliant, but as a teacher, I've met hundreds of kids, and I know a special kid when I see one. Now, let others see it as well, Mia."

I didn't have the heart to look at her, because even though she made me feel better, I didn't want to encourage her. She might decide to have meaningful talks with me every day. Instead, I picked at my cuticles.

"You sound just like a bad talk show host, 'Let your inner beauty shine, next on *The Maureen Fullerton Show.*'"

She stopped untangling my hair and put her hands in her lap.

"You don't have to be so mean to me all the time. It's getting a little old."

Part of me wanted to tell her I was sorry for being so nasty, so she would hold me in her arms and rock me like she used to. But the other part of me wanted to hurt her more so she would immediately leave my bedroom and not come back until I was twenty-one.

I decided to compromise.

"Before you hear about it in the teacher's lounge, I guess I'd better let you know I'm running for ninth grade class president—Lisa nominated me. I know I won't win because I'm running against Cassie Foster, so just let me get through the next week and lose the election graciously. And please, don't make a big deal about this, all right?"

"Oh, honey, that's wonderful!" She hugged me tightly. "I'm so glad you're finally taking a chance in life instead of sitting on the sidelines, waiting for your turn."

I silenced her with my death stare.

"You know my favorite slogan," she continued. "Jump and the net will appear. It looks like it's your turn to jump."

"With my luck," I said, "the net will have a huge hole in it."

"You'll never know unless you jump."

My dad beamed at me across the dinner table. "So, my little princess is running for class president!"

"Mom, I told you not to make a big deal about this!"

"I had to tell your father. We're both so proud of you."

"Speak for yourself," Chris said. "Personally, I think Mia is whacked in the head. There's no way she can beat Cassie Foster for president. Cassie is phat."

"Chris," my dad said, "we don't make fun of people's weight in this house."

"Dad, you're so past it. Cassie's *phat*, not *fat*. Like, she's only the hottest and most popular girl in the freshman class at St. Hilary's. Plus, she has a body that won't quit. Man, I wish there were some chicks like her in my seventh grade class."

"That is enough, Chris," my mom said, spooning another heap of mashed potatoes onto his plate.

I swallowed the last chunk of my meatloaf and asked, "May I be excused?"

"No way! It's your turn to do dishes!" Chris yelled.

"Can we switch and I'll do them tomorrow night?"

"Why? What could you possibly have to do tonight, besides read the dictionary for fun?"

"I'm playing basketball with Tim from next door." I poured on the charm. "So, will you please switch dish duty with me?"

"I'll switch if you give me five bucks."

I rolled my eyes. "No longer are you beneath my contempt."

"I thought you were going to play basketball. Why'd you take a shower?" Chris asked as he pocketed the five bucks from my babysitting stash. "If you're trying to impress Tim with your looks, you'd better forget it. You're so ugly that when you walk into Taco Bell, everyone runs for the border!"

Ignoring him, I slammed the back door behind me.

I shot a few free throws to warm up before I saw Tim cross his backyard. It would've been much easier to hate him if he wasn't so cute.

"Are you feeling better? I can handle a retainer on my shoe, but your dinner landing on me is a whole different story." Tim took the ball from me and made a perfect free throw.

"I've never felt better," I said. "You're not trying to chicken out, are you?"

"No way. Are you ready for total annihilation?"

"Don't bet on it. Play to ten, win by two?" I threw him the ball.

"Should be a quick game, then." Tim tossed me the ball. "You check it."

I took the ball out and as Tim came toward me, I was distracted by the faint scent of cologne. Coming to my senses, I faked left, cross dribbled, and went for a lay-up. This time, I made sure I pushed off with my left foot and followed through—there'd be no retainers flying through the air during this game.

"Nice shot," he said. "Lucky I let you have that one, because that's all you're going to get," Tim said, taking the ball. Dribbling once and stopping, he popped a perfect jump shot to tie the score. "Poetry in motion," he said, tossing me the ball.

"More like motion sickness." I dribbled behind my back so Tim couldn't steal. I cross dribbled again and shot the ball. "Swoosh— nothing but net!" I said.

The game continued point for point. Tim thwarted every trick I knew, but I didn't let him have the advantage. The score was twenty up—neither of us could get the winning two-point edge.

"I heard you're running for class president," Tim panted as he stole the ball from me.

"Yeah, where'd you hear that?" I replied, stealing the ball back and attempting a lay-up. The shot bounced off the rim and Tim rebounded it.

"Cassie called me before dinner. She wants me to work on her campaign. She says she wants fresh ideas," Tim answered, knocking one in from the baseline.

"More like fresh meat," I muttered as I fumbled the rebound.

"What'd you say?" Tim asked, missing his shot.

"I said I think it's great. You two are perfect for each other." I hurled an air ball. "Anyway, Jake Harris might want to help me—he's the one who seconded my nomination."

"Then I guess I'll tell her 'okay'." Tim rebounded the ball and sank the winning shot. "That's it, twenty-two to twenty. Next time I'll play at full speed to shorten your misery."

"Are you always this hostile with everyone you meet?"

"Nah, there's just something special about you. For some reason, I especially enjoy seeing you sweat." Tim smiled, then began whistling *We Are the Champions* as he walked through his yard without a backward glance.

Chapter
Seven

A s the earth towered closer, my classmates lined up along the roller coaster to watch me fly out of control. I heard their raucous laughter grow and grow until it reached a frenzied, high pitched buzz. When my car hit the ground, a terrifying scream escaped my lips. I woke up sweaty and confused as the buzz continued to assault my ears. Struggling for breath, I hit the snooze button and moaned.

"What did I get myself into?" I said.

Lisa was waiting for me at the corner.

"I have great news! Your whole campaign is mapped out."

"I don't have a campaign. All I have is my name on the ballot. We weren't going to make a big deal about this. Remember?"

"Mia, this is your chance to make a difference. If you're class president, you'll have the power to make sure all the ninth graders' voices are heard. If Cassie becomes president, her main goal will be to change the school's colors so they don't clash with her skin tone. Anyway, all the work is done. Mike came over last night and we made some awesome posters to hang in the hallway. He said he would get to school early today to hang them up before class starts."

"Mike is working on my non-existent campaign?"

"As soon as I asked him to help me, he said he'd be right over.

We had the best time together. He's so funny and smart . . . and really cute."

"Are you starting a Mike Finnegan fan club or what?"

"I just like him, all right?"

"Fine, calm down."

"We had such a great time last night, I don't want you to ruin it by making jokes. I mean, the time totally flew by when we were together and we didn't even know how late it was until Mike's mom called, telling him to get home before it got too dark. And then, right before Mike was going to leave—" Lisa paused, her face turning red—"he kissed me!"

"Mike *kissed* you?"

"I hope you don't mind. I know Mike has always been more your friend than mine, but I like him so much, and he's an incredible kisser!"

I tried to picture Lisa and Mike kissing, but it hurt my brain too much.

"I've been hoping for so long that Mike and I would get together, but I never told you because I didn't know how you really felt about him. Then, yesterday, when you told me you'd never like him for more than a friend, I decided to go for it. Oh, Mia, you're the best!"

Lisa pulled me into a hug and I didn't move. I felt like I did when I was ten and walked out of swimming lessons, only to discover my bike had been stolen. It had been there when I left, but when I came out, it was gone. And now it was happening all over again—one minute Mike liked me, and the next, he belonged to someone else. And even though I would never have gone out with Mike in a million years, it had been nice to know he liked me. I just couldn't believe Lisa stole the only guy who'd ever even thought about dating me. I looked at her suspiciously. Maybe she'd also had a hand in stealing my bike.

Oblivious to my lack of enthusiasm, Lisa rambled on as we made our trek to St. Hilary's.

"It doesn't change anything if Mike and I are together. The three of us can still hang out together and have fun. It's not like I'd ever choose hanging out with Mike over you. Nothing's going to change."

Mr. Benson called the class to order.

"As you can tell from the posters in the hallway, we have two excellent candidates running for freshman class president this year—Cassie Foster and Mia Fullerton."

Everyone turned to stare at Cassie and me. I slumped down in my desk while Cassie, looking more gorgeous than usual, smiled so brightly, I almost expected to see sparkles bounce off her pearly white teeth.

"Now, let's talk about other presidents," Mr. Benson continued. "Your assignment this week is to write about who you think was the best president of the United States. Then, you will compose a persuasive essay explaining your choice. Make sure you back up your opinion with facts. Presentations are next Monday, so get busy."

I got out a piece of paper and Mike leaned over and asked, "Do you want to look at some books together?"

I shook my head.

"No, thanks. It's easier for me to do research alone."

"Um," he said, "I was talking to Lisa."

Lisa broke into a wide grin.

"Sure," Lisa said. "That would be great. Just let me gather my stuff."

It took Lisa only fifteen minutes to abandon me. I was definitely going to check her garage for my old bike. I grumbled as I got out of my seat to gather some research books in the back of the classroom.

Tim leaned over my shoulder.

"How's your ego this morning? Feeling a little bruised?"

"Save it. I'm not in the mood."

"Man, are you a sore loser, or are you always this cranky in the morning?"

Blatantly ignoring him, I grabbed a book on presidents. Tim selected the book next to mine.

"So, who are you going to write about?" he asked.

Figuring if I answered him, he might leave me alone, I said, "I don't know, maybe Franklin D. Roosevelt, Jimmy Carter, or Bill Clinton."

"You've got to be joking."

"Why, who are you choosing? Richard Nixon?"

"Exactly."

"Now, you've got to be joking. He was one of the worst presidents of all time." My mom, the flaming liberal, had ranted about Nixon for so long I knew her spiel by heart. "He raised illegal money from companies, forged letters on stolen Democratic Party stationery attacking McGovern, and broke into the Democratic National headquarters at Watergate, where he stole files and planted microphones."

"Richard Nixon was a great international diplomat who ended the Vietnam War. On the other hand, FDR started a welfare system that has our country paying people who choose not to work, Jimmy Carter was a peanut farmer who led the U.S. into a recession, and Bill Clinton never said an honest word in his life. Those guys are great role models."

"For your information, all these 'guys' listened to working class people and made a difference in their lives. They didn't use people solely to advance their own interests, like Nixon did. If I ever become president, I'll be like them and help everyone—not just the rich people!"

Tim clapped his hands in mock appreciation. "If you're through making speeches, I think I'll go back to my seat and read about a truly great leader—Richard M. Nixon."

Grabbing a book on presidents, I stormed over to my seat and furiously searched to find the most liberal president I could. Then, I spent the rest of the period studying John F. Kennedy, because he was Catholic and good looking, and because he beat Richard Nixon in the 1960 election.

I walked into my English classroom and immediately wanted to escape when I saw my mom wearing an aviator's hat and a huge scarf wrapped around her neck. She greeted us by saying, "Good morning. I was wondering if anyone has seen me or my plane. I ask because there are a lot of stories as to what happened to me. My name is Amelia Earhart, and I disappeared over the Pacific Ocean in 1937. Some people think the Japanese captured me. Some think I crashed in the ocean. And some people think I became a housewife in New Jersey. After I tell you about my life, I'll let you decide."

At the end of her dramatization, my mom concluded, "This is the beginning of our Images of Greatness unit. Your culminating project will be to write a speech from the point of view of a famous person. You will work on this assignment throughout the entire unit and it will be worth fifty percent of your grade. You will need to dress as your hero during your presentation to get the highest possible number of points. You have the rest of the period to write, so get to it."

I pulled out a piece of paper and gnawed on the end of my pencil, trying to figure out who to write about. Maybe I'd research Harry Houdini because it would be really handy to know how to make myself disappear until after the election.

Sitting down at my lab table, I took Tim's book, *The Presidency of Richard Nixon*, and placed *JFK: The Man, The Myth, The President* on top of it.

Jake plopped down on his stool. "Hey, dude, your posters are off the heezy for sheezy."

"Thanks—I think."

Cassie climbed onto her stool. "I can't believe you're actually running against me for class president. Just because you got a new look doesn't stop you from being Mia the Meek. I mean, what are you going to do when you have to give a speech in front of the whole class?"

Tim coughed loudly. "'Mia the Meek?' You've got to be kidding."

"You don't know Mia well enough yet," Cassie replied. "She'd rather die than have anyone look at her. Isn't that right, Mia?"

"Well . . ."

"I might have only known Mia for a few days," Tim interrupted, "but 'Mia the Meek' is not the nickname that first comes to mind."

"Quiet chicks rock," Jake said, punching me in the arm.

I instinctively rubbed the spot where his hand had touched me. "Thanks, Jake."

"Dude, me and my dawgs are hanging at the movies Friday night. You wanna chill with us?"

I was momentarily speechless. "Me?" I said finally, as if I was being strangled.

"Jake, we already have it planned," Cassie interrupted, clenching her jaw.

"Mia's fly. She's got game."

"Well, in that case," Cassie replied, "Tim, would you like to come, too?"

Tim shrugged. "Sure. Who all's going?"

"Jessie, Anthony, Collin, and Stephanie. We're meeting at Hillside Theatre in the mall to see whatever's playing around seven."

"Sounds fun. Mia and I live next door to each other, so we can ride together and meet you there."

Sister Donovan interrupted our discussion. "Clean off your tables. We have our first lab today."

Jake leaned over to me.

"So, you're down with it?"

"I guess so," I said, hoping he meant going out with him Friday night.

Cassie put her hand on Tim's.

"We can talk about Friday when you call me tonight," she said.

Sister Donovan stared at us and cleared her throat, so we quickly cleaned off our table.

"Today we are going to do a simple experiment—changing a solid into a liquid and then back again. First, you will melt mothballs in a test tube. You will want to slowly and gently stir the test tube mothballs over the flame because they are highly flammable. We don't want any test tubes breaking. Once the mothballs have melted, you will remove the test tube from the flame, measure its temperature, and put it in cold water to measure at what temperature the mothballs turn solid again. I will be watching to see how you follow directions. Please get started."

"Go get the supplies and I'll set up the lab," Tim ordered.

I put my hands on my hips.

"Who died and made you boss? How about *you* get the supplies and *I'll* set up the lab?"

"Why does it matter?"

"Because I don't like it when you tell me what to do. First, you tell Cassie we'll ride together on Friday night without asking me, and now you're telling me to go get the equipment?"

"You're throwing this fit because I told Cassie we could ride together? It only makes sense to go together—we live next door to each other."

"But what if I don't want to go with you? And what if I was

47

counting on setting up the lab? Did you ever think to ask me before you started acting like the master of the universe?"

Tim heaved a sigh.

"Fine. Why don't we compromise and both get the supplies, and then set up the lab together?"

"All right, but you'd better hurry up because everyone's already started."

"Who's the one wasting time here?"

"I'd say you are," I grumbled, following Tim to the table filled with supplies.

We set up the lab and turned on our Bunsen burner. As I stirred, Tim rolled the mothballs into the test tube filled with warm water. Then, he whispered in my ear, "Could you have salivated any more when Jake asked you out? I think I got a little drool on my sleeve."

"You're depriving a village somewhere of its idiot," I shot back. "Besides, I could've filled a bucket with your slobber when the wicked witch of St. Hilary's asked *you* out."

"I think Cassie is sweet."

"Sweet as strychnine," I muttered, stirring the mothballs in the test tube a bit more vigorously.

"I don't think you're supposed to be stirring the mothballs that hard. Sister Donovan said to gently stir them."

"I told you to stop telling me what to do. I can stir the mothballs as hard as I want!" Using the plastic stirrer, I moved the mothballs around the test tube even more forcefully. "See—it just makes them melt faster."

"It does not. You're going to break the test tube."

"I don't mind you talking, as long as you don't care if I don't listen," I answered.

He tried to grab the stirrer from my hand. "Are you always this stubborn, or are you making a special effort today?"

"Fine, if you think you're so smart, you do it!" As I yanked the stirrer from the test tube, I accidentally shattered the glass. The melted mothballs fell into the flame of the Bunsen burner and a huge ball of fire instantaneously exploded in front of us. The flammable concoction quickly spread across the table and flames followed in its wake.

"Whoa, dude, our table's like, totally on fire," Jake remarked.

The table went up like a pile of kindling and the room soon filled with a cloud of black smoke. The sprinklers on the ceiling kicked in and the fire alarm blared. Students piled out of the room in a panic, practically climbing on top of each other to escape the fumes and stream of water shooting from the ceiling. I guess all of those years of fire drills, marching single file out of the hypothetical flames, didn't do us any good. When a real fire started, it was every man for himself.

Sister Donovan grabbed the fire extinguisher off the wall. Unleashing a spray of white powder across our table, she doused the flames shooting into the air. As the last of the students escaped, she yelled, "Who is responsible for this?"

Feeling like the guilty party, I shouted over the clanging of the alarm, "I'm so sorry, Sister Donovan!"

"It's my fault, Sister Donovan," Tim yelled over me. "I should've watched Mia a little closer—I knew she was doing the experiment wrong."

"*I* was doing it wrong? At least I was doing something—you were just standing there talking!"

"At least I didn't try to burn down the school!"

"I wouldn't have burned down the school if you weren't distracting me!"

"I wouldn't have distracted you if you—"

"Hold it!" Sister Donovan interrupted. "I'm going to run to the office to tell Mrs. Jensen to turn off that blasted alarm. Maybe we can catch the firemen before they head here with their sirens blaring!"

As Sister Donovan scurried out the door, Tim and I stood alone in the room, staring at the aftermath of chaos. A layer of white residue from the fire extinguisher covered the floor and the water spraying down from the sprinklers was turning all the folders and papers into a soggy mess.

Abruptly, the alarm and sprinklers stopped and an eerie silence suddenly descended on us. Without speaking, Tim and I walked around the room, turning off Bunsen burners and picking up lab stools and papers strewn about the floor. I pushed my wet hair out of my face and silently groaned when I looked at our table. The top was charred black and would be impossible to repair. As I looked miserably at Tim, he burst out in laughter.

"I don't see what you could possibly find funny at this moment," I said.

"If I'd known you were going to start a fire, I would've brought some marshmallows," he said.

"Ha ha, very funny."

"Are you sure they call you Mia the Meek? To me, you seem more like Mia the Mighty—faster than a flying retainer, able to burn down science rooms in a single bound. It's a bird, it's a plane. No, it's Mia the Mighty!" Tim started to laugh even harder.

I glared at him, but then the absurdity of the situation overwhelmed me and I burst out in laughter too. The harder I tried to stop, the harder I laughed, and the more I laughed, the more Tim laughed. Soon, tears were streaming down both of our faces and every time one of us tried to stop, we looked at each other and started laughing even harder.

"I'm glad you find this so amusing," a somber Sister Donovan said as she entered the room. "Do you realize your mistake caused the entire school to exit the building? You will both get an F for this lab and I expect you to come in after school every day this week to work off the cost of a new lab table."

I tried to give Sister Donovan my most humble, apologetic face, but I made eye contact with Tim and erupted in laughter again.

"Should I make it two weeks of cleaning the lab?" Sister Donovan said.

I bit the inside of my mouth until I tasted blood. Without looking at Tim, I said in my most respectful voice, "I'm so sorry, Sister Donovan. I don't know why we're laughing. It must be the fumes from the fire."

"I accept your apology. You are dismissed." Sister Donovan walked over to her desk and pulled out a giant aspirin bottle and her rosary. Pouring a small handful of aspirin into her mouth, she stared out the window and began praying. We humbly left the science room with our heads bowed down in shame, but when we reached the hallway, we burst into laughter again.

Tim said, "I think I'm going to start calling you my 'lab partner in crime'."

"I can be Thelma and you can be Louise," I said.

"How about Bonnie and Clyde?"

"As long as I get to be Bonnie."

Tim put his arm around my shoulder.

"Louis, I think this may be the beginning of a beautiful friendship."

"What's that from?" I asked.

"That's the last line from the movie *Casablanca*. Don't tell me you've never seen it."

"No. What's it about?" I said.

"It's only the best movie ever made! It stars Humphrey Bogart and—"

"Oh, it's an old movie. I hate old movies," I said.

"You hate old movies?" Tim stammered. "How is that possible?"

"They're full of dead people," I said. "I like movies that have this amazing new technology called color."

"You have got to be kidding. Let me see if I have time to explain how wrong you are before next period starts."

I rolled my eyes. "I can hardly wait."

Chapter

Eight

The rest of the week was dedicated to fire safety in science class. By the time the bell rang Friday morning, I was exhausted from stopping, dropping, and rolling across the science room floor. On the way to English class, Lisa pointed to one of my campaign posters.

"I can't believe it! Another poster ruined. I'm running out of money buying new poster boards."

I looked at the poster with "Only Mia Can Prevent Science Fires" scribbled on it.

"Lisa," I said, "the election is Monday. I think it's a little too late for damage control. It doesn't matter anyway—I'm not going to win."

"Stop saying that! You have a really good chance of winning this election. A lot of people don't like Cassie. They're just too afraid to tell her."

"Well, they're not going to vote for me. I'm a nobody."

"Wouldn't it feel good to finally come out of the corner you've been hiding in for so many years and actually stand up for something?" Lisa snapped. "I thought you wanted to change, but I guess you're happy being Mia the Meek."

"So, I'm tired of being called Mia the Meek. That doesn't mean I can beat Cassie in the election."

Lisa smiled. "Yes it does. I have a plan."

"Oh great, another plan."

"You ready to go clean the science lab?" Tim asked, popping a handful of M&M's in his mouth. He offered me the bag. "Want some?"

"Sure," I replied, taking a single M&M.

"How can you take just one? You're supposed to eat M&M's in handfuls, not one at a time."

"I believe strongly that less is more."

"That must be true, considering you're going out with Jake tonight," Tim replied, finishing off the bag of candy. "You know, when God was throwing brains down on earth, Jake was holding an umbrella. I, on the other hand was holding a basket. And not only do I have brains, but I'm also blessed with good looks."

"You're right—dark and handsome."

"Really?"

"Yeah. When it's dark, you look handsome. Anyway, Jake more than makes up for his lack of brains with his incredible good looks."

"Oh, so you *do* think he's stupid."

"That's not what I said." I sighed. "Look, do you think there's any way we can spend our last afternoon together without you trying to pick a fight with me?"

Tim held up his hand in a Boy Scout salute.

"I'll be nice—Scout's honor."

Tim held the dust pan as I swept the floor.

"So, what do you think of being an organ donor?"

"Tim, you gave me your Scout's honor."

"Well, the Scout thing doesn't really apply to me because I never was a Boy Scout. I got kicked out after the first meeting because I disagreed with the troop leader over which badge we should earn first. I wanted to learn how to tie knots, and he wanted to teach us how to start a fire by rubbing sticks together. I mean, hadn't he ever heard of matches?"

"All right," I said, "even you can't argue with me on this topic. Of course I'd be an organ donor."

"Are you crazy?" Tim said. "Not me."

"What could you possibly find wrong with being an organ donor?"

"What if you were an organ donor and were in an accident. You had a chance of living, but it was a long shot. So, the doctors don't even take a chance at saving you because they don't want to risk losing your organs. In the end, the doctors remove them, some other person gets to live, and you're toast."

"I hardly think a doctor is going to rip out my heart if I have a chance at living," I said, putting the broom away.

"It happens. I saw it on TV. There's no way anyone's getting my organs."

"You would deny another person's chance at life just because you saw some stupid TV show?"

"It wasn't stupid," Tim said as he started washing test tubes. After a moment of silence, he asked, "So, who do you think is the smartest *Scooby Doo* character?"

I grabbed the test tubes from him and placed them in the rack to dry.

"Velma, of course."

"No way! Scooby Doo is a dog and he can *talk*—he's got to be pretty smart to do that!"

"But Velma always has a plan."

"But Scooby and Shaggy always solve the mystery!"

Sister Donovan walked into the room.

"Are you two still arguing? I will pray to St. Jude, the patron saint of lost causes, that you find some common ground in the future. But for now, you may leave early because I've got plans tonight."

"Thanks, Sister Donovan." Tim grabbed his backpack and took off in a sprint. "Bet I can beat you home, Mia!"

"Does everything have to be a competition with you?" I groaned, grabbing my backpack and running after him.

After dinner, I took a shower and then tried on every outfit I had. I finally decided on some jeans and a cinched V-neck top that showed off what little cleavage I had. After swirling on some flavored Chapstick, I descended the stairs.

My dad snapped a picture.

"I can't believe my little girl is going out on her first date."

"Dad, this isn't the prom. I'm just meeting a guy at the movies."

"I want you to know: if Jake does anything inappropriate, not only can I call his parents, but I can flunk him in English class," my mom warned.

"Mom, I think Jake can flunk English class on his own—he doesn't need your help."

"True, his potential in the literary arts is not great. But he *is* awfully cute," she said, nudging me.

My dad snapped another picture and I spread my hands over my face.

"All right, that's enough. The photo shoot's over. Anyway, I think I hear Tim's parents' car." I waved goodbye and ran out the door.

I climbed into the backseat of the car and couldn't help but notice how cute Tim looked in his polo shirt and jeans. Then I did a mental headslap. I wasn't supposed to be checking out another guy on my first date with someone else, especially when that someone else had been the love of my life for the past five years! I moved as far away from Tim as I could and leaned my head against the window.

Tim scooted over to my side and his breath tickled my neck as he whispered in my ear, "How about a little wager on tonight's date?"

"What kind of wager?" I asked, pushing him back over to his side of the car.

Tim's eyes darted to the front seat to see if his parents were listening, then he lowered his voice.

"If I can get Cassie to kiss me goodnight, you have to make me a batch of cookies."

"What's in it for me?"

"If you get up the courage to kiss Jake goodnight, I'll let you beat me in basketball tomorrow."

"I can already beat you in basketball."

"Yeah, right," Tim smirked. "Well, if you're too scared—"

"I am *not* scared,"I said.

"Then, it's a deal," he said.

"Fine," I muttered, returning my gaze to the car window and wondering what I'd gotten myself into now.

The ending credits rolled and Jessie declared, "That was absolutely the worst movie I've ever seen in my entire life!"

"Girl, you're off your rector. *Robo Destroyer* is poppins," Jake replied as we dumped our empty popcorn containers into the trash bin and headed for the exit.

"Whatever." Jessie looked out the glass door of the lobby. "There's my parents—we gotta get going. Thanks for the movie, Anthony."

Anthony shrugged. "It's all good."

"Yeah, thanks Collin. Call me," Stephanie said as she followed Jessie out the door.

"I can't believe that's all the thanks you guys are going to get,"

Cassie said as her icy blue eyes flashed at Collin and Anthony. "It's a good thing I know how to properly thank a guy for taking me to a movie."

And with that, Cassie grabbed Tim with her claws and began slobbering all over him in a giant make-out session. It was like watching a bad accident, and I couldn't turn away. After what seemed like an eternity of watching gallons of saliva exchange, Cassie finally broke the suction, walked out the lobby without saying another word, and climbed into Jessie's parents' SUV. After it pulled away, Tim turned toward me and flashed an arrogant grin.

I bet that low-down dirty rotten sneak told Cassie about the bet so he could cheat me out of a batch of cookies! Well, there was no way I was going to let him win this time. Giving Tim a defiant stare, I whipped my retainer out of my mouth, gathered every scrap of courage in my nervous body, grabbed Jake, and gave him a kiss he'd remember for the rest of his life. I put into action everything I'd ever read about kissing from my *Young Teen* magazine, and I must have done something right, because Jake enthusiastically responded.

It was everything I'd imagined . . . until Jake's tongue started doing this weird lizard thing and darted in and out of my mouth. I pulled him closer and tried to contain his tongue so Tim wouldn't have anything to make fun of. We were just getting back into the groove when a car horn blared and I pulled away. I looked out the lobby door and saw my parents' faces pressed against their car windows, gawking at me with horrified expressions. *Great, I must be the only person on earth who initiates her adolescent love life with her parents watching from the sidelines.* I slipped my retainer back into my mouth, said goodnight, and ran out to the car.

As Tim and I climbed into the back seat, my mom asked in a quivering voice, "So, did you have good time?"

Tim smirked. "It looks like Mia did."

I nudged him hard and looked out the window, but I couldn't help but smile. They couldn't call me Mia the Meek any more.

My parents marched me inside and sat me down on the living room couch.

"What do you have to say for yourself?" my mom demanded.

"That the cop in *Robo Destroyer* is a very good defender of truth and the American way?"

"I am talking about your very public display of affection."

"I think it would be a good idea if you don't make any big plans for tomorrow," my dad added.

"I'm grounded Saturday just because I kissed a guy? You're so lame. For God's sake, I'm almost fifteen."

"We just think it would be a good idea if you stay home tomorrow and reflect on your behavior," my mom said wearily. "And please, do not take the Lord's name in vain in this household."

"Whatever. Can I go now?" I asked, rolling my eyes as far up as they could go without hurting myself.

"We'll continue this discussion tomorrow," my dad called as I ran up the stairs to my bedroom.

I raced into my room, dove onto my bed, and pushed speed dial for Lisa's number. I gave Lisa the whole story, deciding to leave out Jake's impersonation of a frog catching a fly.

"So, what did it feel like? Did you see stars?" she asked.

I didn't know how to respond. I'd been so focused on proving to Tim that I could kiss someone that I hadn't even thought about stars.

Lisa interrupted the silence.

"Was he a good kisser? When Mike first kissed me, I felt a tingle from my head to my toes. Did your body tingle?"

"It felt good, but I think I was so busy showing off for Tim that I didn't have time to tingle."

"Mia, you're too much. When you're kissing, you're supposed to be thinking about the guy in your arms, not someone else!"

"Who cares who I was thinking about? All that matters is that I got my first kiss tonight and it was with Jake Harris!" I heard a distinct *click* as my mom picked up the extension, so I said, "Lisa, I've got to go. I'm grounded tomorrow, but I'll call you on Sunday." After Lisa hung up, I said into the phone, "You can hang up now too, Warden."

I hung up the phone, turned off the lights, and settled into bed. Then, closing my eyes, I tried to relive the experience of Jake's lips on mine. Did I feel tingly? I racked my brain, but in the end, all I could remember was the satisfaction I felt not losing the bet with Tim. Maybe Lisa was right. If I was thinking about Tim when I kissed Jake, did my first real kiss even count?

Chapter
Nine

I woke up early Saturday morning so I could sneak out of the house for a quick run. I didn't think being grounded meant I couldn't get some exercise, but I didn't want to wait around to ask. Sometimes, it was easier to assume the boundaries of my parents' rules rather than actually ask for them. That way, I could plead ignorance if and when I got busted.

The temperature was a cool sixty-five degrees, and the air possessed a distinct smell, declaring fall was coming. The leaves were transforming into various shades of orange, red, and yellow and they fluttered under the clear, aqua-colored sky. My heart was full from the beauty of the day and thoughts of Jake.

I'd just reached my turn-around point at the duck pond when I saw Maggie running toward me, so I stopped to wait for her. Sprinting to the pond, she asked, without even a hint of being winded, "How's the election going?"

"Don't ask," I panted. "Lisa seems to think I can win, but she's the only one."

"At least I'll be able to vote for someone I like this year. When we were at Assumption, only the popular kids got to be class president. There wasn't anyone like you even running for office." Maggie quickly added, "I didn't mean it like that."

"Me not being popular is hardly a news flash."

"But you're nice. And I know all the freaks and geeks in the ninth grade class are voting for you. If you think about it, there's way more of us than there are popular kids, so maybe you do have a chance of winning."

"Maybe I should change my slogan to 'Mia the Meek, Queen of the Freaks.'"

"I like it—it's catchy."

"Well, I better get home." I pretended to modestly shuffle the ground with my foot. "My parents grounded me for absolutely no reason . . . other than I kissed Jake Harris last night!"

Maggie screamed. "No way!"

"Yes way, but I'll have to tell you all about it at school on Monday. I really am grounded and I need to get home before anyone wakes up," I said, turning to make my way home.

I ran as fast as I could, which isn't saying much, but unfortunately, I wasn't quick enough, because when I tiptoed in the back door, my parents were already at the kitchen table drinking coffee and reading the paper. My mom looked up.

"Well, since you have so much energy this morning, I made a list of jobs for you to do. Go take your shower and get busy."

By four o' clock, I'd finished my last task—re-arranging the Tupperware drawer—and gone in search of my mom. I found her sprawled on the family room floor, corrected papers surrounding her. I put my hands on my hips.

"I'm finished with everything on your list. Is there anything else you need me to do, like clean the bathroom floor with my toothbrush?"

She put down the paper she was correcting and rubbed her eyes.

"I'm tired of fighting with you. Let's call a truce. Why don't you get cleaned up and we can all go out to dinner together as a special treat?"

"Oh joy, I can't imagine anything more fun than going out to dinner with *my family*." I plopped down on the couch. "Can you pretty please take me to a restaurant that has a kiddie menu and crayons so I can connect the dots as I wait for my meal?"

"That comment just got you grounded for Sunday as well," my mom said, climbing up off the floor. "While your father and I take Chris out to dinner, I suggest you start researching your final project in English, or you'll be repeating my class in summer school."

"What am I supposed to eat for dinner?"

"I think there's some microwave popcorn in the cupboard."

"I'm supposed to starve just because I don't want to go out to eat with you?" I crossed my arms over my chest. "And I can't work on my report because I don't even know who I'm going to write about."

"Since you're acting like such a martyr, why don't you write about Joan of Arc?"

I scowled. "That's perfect," I said. "Her parents lived in the dark ages, too."

Sunday afternoon, I whispered into the phone, "Lisa, it's me, Mia."

"Who?"

"It's me, Mia."

"Speak up, I can't hear you."

I whispered louder, "It's Mia."

"Is this an obscene phone call? Because if it is, you're not doing a very good job—I can barely hear you."

I whispered even louder, "It's Mia!"

"Mia, what's wrong? Why are you whispering?"

"I'm not supposed to be on the phone. Look, this is the first chance I've had all day to call you and I just wanted you to know that I'm not coming over today to write my speech for the election.

My parents extended my grounding."

"What did you do? Make out with the mailman?"

"Very funny."

"Don't worry about it," Lisa said. "I've already written a speech for you. Listen to this, 'Four score and seven years ago, our fathers brought forth on this continent a new nation, conceived in liberty, and dedicated to the proposition that all men are created equal—'"

"Uh, Lisa, I think that speech has been done before."

"No good? How about I start the speech with, 'I have a dream' and end it with 'Free at last! Free at last! Thank God almighty, we are free at last!'?"

"I think I'm in big trouble."

"I'm kidding. Actually, I have a really good speech already written. My plan is to have you give such an amazing address that everyone will *have* to vote for you. All you have to do is practice it. I'll bring it over later."

"You're the best," I said.

My mom yelled from downstairs, "Mia, are you on the phone?"

"Lisa, I've got to go. The guard discovered I'm communicating outside the prison walls."

I hung up the phone and walked downstairs. Grabbing an apple from the fruit bowl on the counter, I said, "I was talking to Lisa about my speech tomorrow, if you care."

My mom mimicked my tone of voice.

"Well, *if you care*, your father needs help cleaning out the garage and washing the car, so get out there."

I sighed as heavily as I could so my mom would realize how unfunny she was. Then I threw my apple back in the bowl and ambled outside. My dad, in the middle of hauling everything out of the garage, stopped when he saw me.

"Great! I could use a helper."

"I'm not a helper, but a convict assigned to the chain gang."

"Well, whatever you are, you and your brother need to wash the van." He threw me an empty bucket.

"Do I have to wash the van with him? I'd rather be in solitary confinement."

"I heard that, dog breath!" Chris yelled, turning on the hose, soaking me from head to toe, and running from what he knew would be my wrath.

"Get back here, you gene mutation!" I screamed, grabbing the dropped hose. I filled the bucket and began chasing him around the front yard.

Chris dodged the bucket of water I tossed in his direction.

"You'll never catch me—I've seen you run before. Grandma Fullerton runs faster than you!"

I dropped the bucket and grabbed the hose. Tackling Chris to the ground, I put my finger over the nozzle and gave him a full spray in the face.

"I let Grandma win because I'm her favorite," I said. "Now you have to answer: who's your favorite sister?"

"Get off me!" Chris sputtered.

"Say it!" I yelled, holding the water closer to his face.

"All right, Mia's my favorite sister!"

I dropped the hose and let him up. Chris immediately yelled at the top of his lungs, "Mia's my favorite sister who stuffs her bra with socks!" and took off around the back of the house.

"Jerk!" I yelled, chasing him to the backyard. "I do not stuff my bra with socks!"

"Hi, Mia," came a familiar voice. I stopped dead in my tracks and turned toward Tim's deck. "Isn't it sweet that Mia still plays with her little brother?" Cassie said to Tim. "It must be hard not having any friends."

I gritted my teeth and headed to my house.

"By the way," Cassie called, "if you really do stuff your bra, you should get bigger socks, because nobody can tell."

I suddenly became very aware of the wet T-shirt clinging to my flat chest. As I opened the back door to my house, Cassie yelled, "Tim's helping me write my speech for tomorrow. Too bad Jake couldn't help you write yours. But then again, Jake has trouble with any words over two syllables."

I couldn't take it any more. I turned around and said, "But sometimes, all it takes is two syllables. In fact, I have a really simple two syllable phrase that can be summed up with just one finger. Want to see it?"

My mom's voice boomed behind me.

"Mia Claire Fullerton, get in here NOW!"

I slammed the back door and stormed into the kitchen.

"What has gotten into you?" my mom bellowed. "First, we catch you making out with Jake, and now I catch you about to use an obscene gesture?"

"If you'd let me finish, you would've seen I was going to give Cassie the thumbs up sign. You know, good luck on your speech tomorrow, may the best person win—a gesture of peace and love . . ."

"I'm not that gullible. Go up to your room and reflect on your behavior this weekend."

"Mom, if I do any more reflecting, I'm going to have to enter the convent. And, for your information, I wasn't 'making out' with Jake—I was winning a bet. Why don't you lay off, for God's sake. And yes, I used the Lord's name in vain, so I guess I can go and reflect on that, too!"

I ran up to my room, slammed the door, and threw myself on my bed. Grabbing a miniature basketball off the floor, I hurled it against the wall. *Wham!* That's for my parents, who won't let me grow up. *Wham!* That's for Chris, who's the biggest imbecile in the world. *Wham!* That's for Cassie, who's a wicked witch. *Wham!* That's for Tim, for helping Cassie and not me. *Wham!*

"Mia, stop that racket or you'll be grounded for a month!" my mom shouted.

I threw the ball one more time. *Wham!* Then I fell back on my bed and began planning torturous punishments for all of them. I'd just reached torture idea one hundred and sixty-seven when I suddenly found myself strapped in my roller coaster car. I began the gradual ascent up the gargantuan hill and then, at the top, plunged into darkness. I screamed, but my voice came out, "Beep! Beep! Beep!"

I groggily reached over and shut off my alarm. I yawned and stretched.

"Man, I've never had a nightmare in the middle of a nap before."

Then it hit me. My alarm wouldn't have gone off in the afternoon. I quickly looked at the clock. It was 6:30 a.m., and I hadn't even looked at my speech for the election!

Chapter
Ten

I raced to my parents' bedroom.

"How could you let me sleep for fifteen hours?"

My mom crawled out of bed. "Honey, you were so exhausted, we didn't have the heart to wake you last night. You must've needed the sleep."

"What I needed was to practice my speech for today's election!"

"Lisa dropped the speech off late yesterday afternoon," Mom said, "but I figured your sleep was more important."

"Well, you figured wrong as usual. Mr. Benson told us we had to memorize our speeches, and now there's no way I'll have time to do that. I'm going to make a total fool of myself today and it's going to be your fault!"

I ran into the bathroom and took a shower in record time. After quickly drying off, I slipped on my lucky underwear and my favorite uniform blouse and skirt. I threw my hair in a ponytail and brushed my teeth as I dashed downstairs. I looked frantically for the notes.

"Where are dey?" I screamed, my mouth full of toothpaste.

"What are you talking about?" my mom yelled from upstairs.

"The dotes! The dotes Lisa left for my speech!"

"If you're talking about a stack of note cards," Chris yelled, "they're here on the kitchen table. I spilled some milk on them."

I ran to the kitchen sink, spit out my toothpaste, and grabbed the notes, drying them off on my skirt.

"Thanks a lot, moron."

Chris shoved cereal in his mouth.

"Who's the moron? You can't even write your own speech," he said, spraying Frosted Flakes along the kitchen table.

I hurriedly scanned the notes.

"I can't memorize all this! There are too many words with too many syllables, and too little time to look up each word in the dictionary!"

My mom came into the kitchen and poured herself a cup of coffee.

"You'll be fine. Just say what's in your heart. You don't need a speech written by somebody else."

Chris poured more cereal into his bowl.

"Yeah, the only thing that could save you is if you *were* somebody else."

Lisa opened her locker and pulled out her American History textbook.

"Were you really sleeping when I came over yesterday?"

"Yeah, I slept for fifteen hours last night. I haven't done that since I was six months old."

"So, what did you think of my speech?"

I paused.

"Um, I know you're really smart and everything, but did you have to use such big words? For example," I said, looking at my notes, "'Cassie Foster is the platitudinous candidate?' I don't even know what 'platitudinous' means."

"It means that she's trite."

"And that means . . ."

"It means she's old news—you know, a has-been."

"Shouldn't I talk about myself rather than put Cassie down?

Look at this part of the speech—you tell them to 'ratiocinate and vote for me'. I can't even pronounce it, let alone ask my classmates to do it!"

"'Ratiocinate' means to make the most logical choice—I thought everybody knew that." Lisa sighed. "I worked very hard on this speech and spent a lot of time making sure every word was perfect. *I* was busy working while *you* were busy sleeping."

"You know I'm grateful for all your hard work," I said, "but sometimes you forget that nobody is as smart as you. I'm giving this speech to ninth graders. They won't know what I'm saying when I tell them I'm an 'aspirant' for the ninth grade presidency. They'll think I'm speaking a foreign language!"

"Just memorize the speech, you'll be fine. Quit showing your poltroonery."

"As a reminder," Mr. Benson said, "the assembly for the ninth graders is in the auditorium today at one-thirty. Jessie Carson and Dave Howard are running for vice president, and Mia Fullerton and Cassie Foster are competing for the position of president. I want you to listen to the speeches and make your decision based on who you think would be best for the job. Remember, they'll be running your class government. Now, let's move on to the other presidential speeches that are due today. Who would like to go first?"

"Mr. Benson?" Cassie asked in a voice so sweet I felt like I needed to brush my teeth. "I brought some cherry lollipops for my speech on George Washington, because everyone knows he never told a lie, even when he chopped down the cherry tree. Is it all right if I pass them out to the class?"

"I'm always open to a little sugar in the morning. Go ahead, as long as I get the first one." Mr. Benson reached into the bag, then popped a sucker in his mouth.

I leaned over to Lisa and whispered, "She's bribing the class! That's so unfair . . . why didn't I think of it first?"

Jake strode over to our newly purchased science table and leaned toward me until he was inches from my face.

"Did you get clocked by your units Friday night? I would've called you, but your betty is bunk. She won't, like, flunk me for jocking you, will she?"

My heart began tap dancing in my chest as I felt Jake's breath on my lips.

"Um," I stammered, "my parents grounded me for the weekend, but I'm sure my mom isn't mad at you. She saves all her hostility for me."

"So, you want to chill with me again?"

"Sure." I blushed so hard it hurt.

"If you two are finished," Tim said, poking me in the ribs, "would you please shut up? Sister Donovan is talking and I really need to improve my grade because *somebody's* mistake got me an F on my first lab."

By lunchtime, I hadn't even looked at my speech, so I ducked out of the cafeteria and snuck into my mom's classroom for a quiet cram session. I opened her bottom desk drawer, pulled out a strawberry Pop Tart, and looked at the speech Lisa had written.

"There is no way I'll ever remember all this," I mumbled, spilling Pop Tart out of my mouth. Spying a marker, I sighed. "Desperate times call for desperate measures." Starting with the pinkie finger of my left hand, I copied the entire speech until it ended perfectly on my right pinkie.

Mr. Grizzling heaved himself out of his seat and began walking up and down the rows, placing laminated cards on each student's desk as he passed.

"Every year, I give the Quadratic Formula to my ninth grade students, just as my ninth grade math teacher did for me. I want you to keep this card on your person wherever you go in life, because you never know when this amazing equation will be of assistance to you."

"Thank you, sir," I mumbled as I looked at the card.

$$x = \frac{-b \pm \sqrt{b^2 - 4ac}}{2a}$$

I shoved it into my folder and Cassie raised her hand.

"Mr. Grizzling, I couldn't help but notice that Mia has some-thing written all over her hands. Doesn't rule number four on your list specifically state that there are not to be any marks on anything in the room, other than on our papers?"

"Ms. Fullerton, show me your hands," Mr. Grizzling demand-ed.

I held them out, timidly, for his inspection.

"No student enters my room looking like a walking billboard. Go wash your hands, and don't return until they're spotless."

Reluctantly, I got out of my seat and went to the restroom to wash my hands. Of course, I'd used permanent marker, so by the time my speech had been scrubbed away, so had a layer of my skin. I dried my hands on the sandpaper-soft paper towels the school pro-vided us while I tried to finagle a new way to learn Lisa's speech. It was no use. My brain had moved to a point beyond panic, just one step away from hysteria.

I sat down in a chair next to the other candidates on the stage in the auditorium. My heart was pounding so hard, I was sure I would need CPR by the end of this fiasco. As the rest of the students shuffled into their seats, Mrs. Jensen approached the candidates. She glared at us with her faded blue eyes.

"There will not be any tomfoolery, understand?"

I solemnly nodded my head, afraid to speak—if I opened my mouth, I knew I would throw up.

After that, I must have lapsed into a fog of fear, because the next thing I knew, Mrs. Jensen was poking me in the arm.

"What are you waiting for?" she said. "Get up there."

I looked at her, curious.

"Don't the vice presidential candidates speak first?"

"They just finished," she said, cocking an eyebrow back at me. "What were you doing up here—taking a nap?"

I looked over at Cassie, who was already standing up. How could I have missed Jessie and Dave's speeches? I was going to use them as the basis for making up my own address. Sensing I wasn't going to stand up willingly, Mrs. Jensen grabbed my arm, pulled me out of my seat, and propped me up next to Cassie.

"I won't be able to stay and listen to your speeches because I'm already late for a meeting with the Bishop," she said. "But, believe me, I'll hear about it if you two don't behave yourselves."

As we watched Mrs. Jensen totter off the stage, Cassie whispered to me, "I want to go first."

Feeling like a prisoner receiving a stay of execution, I happily stepped back as Cassie strode over to the microphone. But rather than starting her speech, she instead smiled seductively at the crowd and began unbuttoning her uniform blouse! Before I could react, she had already ripped off her uniform skirt, which must have been rigged with Velcro, revealing a cheerleading outfit consisting of a short skirt and an off-the-shoulder midriff top. After she tossed her clothes into the audience, Stephanie threw her two pompons.

I stood in stunned amazement while Cassie did a back flip hand-spring. Then she grabbed her pompons and cheered, "I've got spirit. Yes I do! I've got spirit. How 'bout you?"

Unable to resist the cheerleading dare to proclaim their own spirit, everyone yelled, "We've got spirit. Yes we do! We've got spirit. How 'bout you?" An auditorium full of fingers pointed back to Cassie, who immediately did three cartwheels and an arial.

"A vote for me is a vote for spirit!" she cheered, ending her routine in a straddle split with her hands in the air.

The audience erupted in cheers as Mr. Benson jumped up on the stage and quickly escorted Cassie out of the auditorium, leaving me alone in the middle of anarchy. A bunch of students yelled, "We want more! We want more! We want more!" And I began praying for a miracle.

The teachers hastily moved among the rows, threatening students with detention if they didn't quiet down, and soon the auditorium was quiet. More than two hundred sets of eyes turned toward me and an expectant hush fell over the room. I unglued my tongue from the top of my mouth, stepped up to the microphone, and cleared my throat.

"If you don't mind, I'm going to leave all my clothes on."

A series of boos erupted from the back of the auditorium, but were quickly silenced by a teacher. I opened my mouth and words began to fall out.

"Um, I'm running for class president because my best friend thought I could make a difference in our school. And before today, I didn't believe her. But as I stood on this stage watching all of you, I suddenly realized that I do have what it takes to be a good president because I am one of you. I mean, not many of us are really popular or able to look good while doing a cheerleading routine. But that doesn't mean we're unimportant." I took a deep breath, not knowing what was going to come out of my mouth next.

"Everyone in our class adds something to it. Just imagine that we're all a part of a giant quilt. What if our quilt only consisted of fancy patches? We wouldn't have a blanket. We'd have a pile of fluff. In order to make a quilt, we need durable patches that can last over time. We need unusual patches that can give the quilt life. We need soft patches that can make the quilt more comfortable. We even need a few beautiful patches to accent it and make it more elegant. When you put all of us together, we can create a masterpiece. So, if you vote for me, I promise to make St. Hilary's into a school that represents all of us and uses everyone's talents. Because if all our voices are heard, we can make our class the best freshman class in the history of St. Hilary's!"

I glanced at Maggie, sitting in the second row.

"So, if you want your voice heard, you must vote for me, Mia the Meek, Queen of the Freaks!"

Dead silence filled the air as I stepped away from the podium. *Oh my God, where did all that come from? Queen of the Freaks? Did I actually say that out loud? And a quilt? I don't even know how to sew on a button!* I eyed the exit sign and began planning my escape to a remote, uninhabited island, when suddenly I heard a few faint claps from the back of the auditorium. These claps quickly grew into thunderous applause and I looked up from my clenched hands to see the entire freshman class on its feet, giving me a standing ovation!

I hastily rushed off the stage and Lisa enveloped me into a bear hug, shouting over the din of students, "What happened to my speech?"

I smiled sheepishly. "It got washed down the drain."

"Good! Your speech was much better!" Lisa laughed as we joined the herd of students making an exodus for the auditorium doors. I felt my mom's hand on my arm as she pulled me aside.

"See? You jumped and you didn't even need a net."

I smiled at her. It didn't matter if I won or lost. The world felt amazing outside of my corner.

Chapter
Eleven

I loaded the last of the dinner dishes into the dishwasher and then, still buzzing from my day, headed outside to shoot a few hoops. I was just warming up when I heard someone call, "You are in desperate need of an expert to teach you how to handle that ball."

I went for a lay-up over Tim's head.

"If an expert comes by," I said, "let me know."

Tim rebounded the ball and dribbled to the perimeter for an outside shot.

"I've been waiting for that batch of cookies you owe me."

"You didn't win the bet. It was a tie."

"Then I guess it's all right for me to beat you in a game."

His shot clanked off the rim. I grabbed the rebound and swished a shot. "In your dreams," I said.

Tim checked the ball and asked, "So, what did you think of Cassie's speech?"

"I thought it was intellectually stimulating. It must have taken you all of five minutes to help her write that yesterday," I said, blocking Tim's shot and stealing the ball. Dribbling around the court, I mimicked, "I've got a body. Yes I do. I've got a body, so I'll show it to you!"

"Hey, don't blame me for that speech—I had nothing to do with it," Tim said, covering me. "Cassie must've thought of it after she left my house. I was just as shocked as you when she started taking off her clothes."

"Don't tell me you didn't enjoy Cassie's speech."

"I didn't say I didn't enjoy it."

I head-faked Tim and drove for a lay-up. "You're such a pig," I said after my bucket.

"No, I'm not. I'm normal. Statistically, the average male thinks about women once every seven seconds."

"No wonder you're so mental. You spend way too much time thinking about girls."

"There's no such thing as 'too much time' when girls are involved," Tim remarked as he grabbed the ball. "By the way, how'd you ever come up with the idea for your speech?"

"It just kind of came to me as I stood up on the stage. Did it sound totally lame?"

Tim dribbled around the court.

"Well, it did get kind of weird when you called yourself 'Queen of the Freaks,' but the rest was pretty original. What gets me is the whole 'Mia the Meek' thing. I just don't get it—you're about as timid as a tidal wave."

"Believe me, I never thought that within a couple weeks of starting high school, I'd be giving a speech to be class president." As Tim dribbled behind his back, I lunged for the ball but missed.

"My charm and award-winning personality must have rubbed off on you."

"If anything of yours rubbed off on me, I'd need to be vaccinated." I grabbed the ball out of Tim's hand and an electric shock snapped my hand. I dropped the ball and rubbed my palm on my shorts.

"Man," Tim said, "did you see that spark? I had no idea you were so hot for me."

"Don't flatter yourself. The only attraction I feel toward you is the urge to beat you in a basketball game, so I can wipe that smug look off your face. Unfortunately, your humiliation on the court will have to wait. I've got a ton of homework tonight." I started walking toward my house.

"Hey, Mia?" I stopped and turned to look at him. "Good luck tomorrow. I hope the best person wins."

Before morning announcements, Mr. Benson gave a predictable speech on how all the candidates were winners and, no matter who became president, would still be contributing members to the class. We nodded our heads in agreement, but secretly we all knew his words didn't mean a thing.

Suddenly, the speakers of the PA system came to life and the air was filled with the sound of Mrs. Jenson loudly blowing her nose.

"I told you to wait to turn on the intercom until I was done clearing my nasal passages!"

The speakers went dead, then squealed as Mrs. Jensen shouted, "Well, I'm done now. Turn it back on! The intercom's on? Why didn't you tell me sooner—oh, never mind." After an additional series of coughing fits, retching sounds, and phlegm clearing, she finally began the morning announcements, "Ladies and gentlemen, the following students will be your class officers for student council this year." She coughed. "This blasted cold! I knew I shouldn't have shaken hands with the Bishop yesterday—he was sniffling all over the place. I need a cough drop." Then there was dead silence as the intercom was turned off.

Just as abruptly, it buzzed to life again and Mrs. Jensen repeated, "The following students will be your class officers: for the freshman class, the vice president will be Jessie Carson, and the president will be . . ." The microphone squealed again, and then there was silence.

"What happened?" Lisa asked.

"Somebody run to the office and check," Mr. Benson commanded.

"I will," Mike yelled, sprinting out the door.

"I hope she didn't die," I whispered to Lisa. "Then we'll never know who won."

"Your concern for her health brings a tear to my eye," Lisa said.

After a few minutes, Mike finally reappeared.

"Mrs. Jensen's cough drop got stuck in her throat."

"Is she all right?" Mr. Benson asked.

"Yeah, Mrs. Peterbody—the secretary—gave her the Heimlich maneuver and it popped right out. Mrs. Peterbody must be stronger than she looks."

Cassie stood up. "Enough about those two geezers, you idiot! Who won?"

Mike smiled. "You can't call me an idiot any more, because I happen to be a good friend of the freshmen class president—Mia, you won!"

There had to be a mistake. But the intercom sprang to life again and Mrs. Jensen announced in a raspy voice, "The freshman class president will be Mia Fullerton."

The class erupted in cheers and we missed hearing the names of the other classes' presidents, but it really didn't matter. I'd won! I sat in a stupor as our American History class ticked away, and jumped up out of my chair when the ending bell rang. In a trance, I gathered my books.

Jake ran over and slapped me on the back, knocking the wind out of me.

"Boo-yah! You're the top dawg!"

I struggled to catch my breath. "Huh?"

"Dude, you're the prez. You wanna chill at my crib tonight? My video games are all that."

"Um, sure. I'll ask my mom next period to see if it's all right."

"Mia," Mr. Benson interrupted, "I need to speak with you and Jessie for a moment."

Jake swaggered out of the class. "I'm out. Holla back later, dude."

Mr. Benson smiled at us. "Well, girls, it looks like the people have spoken. Isn't democracy great? Anyway, here's your list of responsibilities. Mia, as president of the freshman class, you're now in charge of the student store, which includes getting students to work it, ordering supplies, and keeping track of inventory."

"All right," I replied, taking a look at the list of items sold.

"You must order school sweatshirts ASAP. Hoodies are really popular right now and we're running low, so order them today."

I took a catalog from him, thinking: What's a hoodie?

"Next, you need to arrange all the student council meetings. Here's a calendar of extra-curricular events going on for the year. You have to work around all the teachers' meetings, sport practices, academic practices, band practices, play rehearsals, and religious education classes."

"All right," I said more hesitantly.

"OK, let's move on. Here are the ideas that were put in our suggestion box last year—all the things students want the student council to do to raise funds, boost morale, and show leadership. You need to go through this pile and eliminate all suggestions that are vile, ludicrous, or against the law. If you have any suggestions that survive these three categories, organize them in order of importance and begin researching them." Mr. Benson handed me a large box overflowing with scraps of paper.

"Are you sure I have to do all this?" I asked. "What about the other class presidents?"

"I've found I can rely on freshmen to get the job done. Juniors and seniors are too busy with jobs and applying to colleges, and sophomores—well, don't even get me started on them." Mr. Benson shook his head. "Being president of the freshman class is a big responsibility. Are you sure you're up to it?"

I looked at Jessie. I didn't want her telling Cassie I was having second thoughts. I nodded my head more confidently than I felt. "I'm up for the job."

"Good. Now, the last item is probably the most important. As you know, freshmen aren't allowed to go to any of the formal dances at St. Hilary's, so every year we plan a fall and spring informal dance for the freshman class in an effort to let the kids have some fun and also raise money for the student council. Our first dance is in October, which means you have less than one month to get a DJ, buy concession items, hire a security guard, and create a theme. But for now, just get yourself to your next class."

The bell rang and as everyone piled out of the English classroom, my mom rushed over to me.

"Oh, Mia, it seems like just yesterday you were toddling around with a pacifier in your mouth, wearing droopy diapers. Now you're class president!"

I knew the *Petey and the Potty* story would come next, so I decided to get my mom off the track of diaper stories and take full advantage of her warm feelings toward me.

"Mom, can I ask you a huge favor?"

"Of course! How can I deny my little madam president?"

"Can I go over to Jake's house tonight? I promise his parents will be home and I'll get all my schoolwork done before I go. Please, please, please?"

The smile faded from her face.

"Why does your first boyfriend have to be Jake Harris?"

"Mom, Jake's not my *boyfriend,* but he is the most popular guy in our class and he's finally noticed I'm alive."

"Well, if it took him this long to notice I have the most amazing daughter, he's dumber than I thought."

"Mom, you can't call your students dumb."

"I can call my students anything I want, especially if they're dating my daughter." I gave her my most pitiful look and she sighed. "All right, you can go over from seven until nine, but only if his parents are home."

"Thanks, Mom. You're the best!" I hugged her and ran out the door to science class.

After I plopped down on my stool, Jake leaned across the table. "What's up, dude?"

"My mom said 'yes.' I'll be over at seven o'clock, but I have to leave at nine."

"Fo shizzle, I can't wait to be kicking it with my chassy."

Tim whispered in my ear, "If I were you, I'd bring a dictionary tonight. Maybe you can teach him to speak English while you're 'kicking it.'"

My smile didn't dim. "Not even you, Tim Radford, can get me down today."

"Why? What's so great about today?" Cassie asked, filing her nails with the miniature manicure kit she kept in her folder. I bit my lip.

"I'm sorry," I said. "I shouldn't have said that in front of you. I guess you're pretty disappointed about not winning, huh?"

"God, you *are* a freak. I couldn't care less about winning the election. I just thought it'd be fun to do my cheerleading routine in front of my friends. Personally, I'm glad I didn't win. Who wants to do all that work for Mr. Benson? If he were a real teacher, he wouldn't have to get a job in a Catholic school—no offense toward your mom or anything," Cassie added, putting her manicure kit away.

Sister Donovan plopped two dead frogs on our lab table, saving me from saying something I'd regret.

"We are beginning our unit on life sciences, and the best way to immerse you into nature is to explore the miracle of anatomy. We will use these frogs as our gateway to the body."

Jake grabbed his frog and made it tap dance around the table.

"Dude, watch the toad giggin'."

"Jake, put that frog down or I'm going to puke," Cassie said, holding a Kleenex over her nose. For once, I agreed with her.

"I'm protesting this experiment," I declared. "That frog didn't do anything to deserve being cut up by us."

"Forget the protest," Tim replied. "We need this grade, and you're not going to blow it due to your liberal, misguided, bleeding heart, PETA ideals."

"I don't have a bleeding heart. I just don't think we need to cut up helpless amphibians for a school project."

"If you were twice as smart," Tim said, "you'd still be stupid."

Sister Donovan intervened.

"Mia and Tim, are you fighting again? If I had any sense, I'd separate you and assign you to different lab partners."

I gathered my books. "That would be wonderful," I said.

"But since I think you two need to work it out, I'm keeping you together. So, figure out a way to get along, and do it now!"

She walked away and I sat back down on my stool and crossed my arms.

"Fine. Sister Donovan can make me work with you, but she can't make me talk to you."

"You're not going to talk to me?" Tim smiled. "That's the best thing I've heard all day."

Chapter
Twelve

My dad and I pulled into Jake's circular driveway and I looked at his gigantic house. It was not actually "in the hood," as Jake pretended it was, but in the old money part of the city. In fact, I think the governor's mansion was just down the street. My dad turned off the ignition.

"So, what are you and Jake planning on doing tonight?"

"I don't know. Stuff, I guess."

"What sort of 'stuff'?"

"What's your point?"

"Um," Dad said, searching for the right words. "I just remember when I was in ninth grade and, well . . ."

"Dad, if you're going to tell me about your teenage love life, please stop. I already have bad enough nightmares as it is—I don't need you adding to them."

"All right, I get your point. I just want you to know that you don't have to change the way you are just to make someone like you. I think you're pretty likeable already."

"Great—just what every girl wants to hear. I'm the type of girl only a father could love," I muttered, climbing out of the car. My dad opened his car door and I turned to face him. "Oh my God," I said. "You can't walk me to the door. Get back in the car this instant!"

He paused and then, shaking his head, got back into the car. I waited to make sure he didn't follow me, then rang Jake's doorbell, half-expecting a butler named Jeeves to answer the door.

Instead, Jake swung open the door and I suddenly felt very over-dressed as I surveyed his outfit—sweats and a ripped T-shirt. Hearing my dad's engine, I turned around and waved him off. Jake and I watched him pull away.

"So, you wanna chill in the basement?"

"Sure." I followed him downstairs and was soon immersed in a collection of video games, DVDs, CDs, sporting equipment, and posters of half-dressed women draped across the hoods of cars.

"You wanna play a video game?" Jake asked.

"Um, sure, but I don't own any video games, so you'll have to teach me how to play."

"No games? That sucks. I betcha watch a ton of TV."

"Actually, I don't watch a lot of TV, either."

"Dude, what do you do when you're kicking it?"

"I read a lot."

"That's why you're so freakin' smart." Jake popped in a cartridge. "This game's off the hook. Just get your dude through the jungle before the aliens cap him. You have to dodge the jungle dudes and the space dudes. If you see any warrior spears, collect them. You, like, get extra points for those and you can use them to spear all the dudes later in the game. Are you cool with that?"

"Um, I think so."

"You go first," he said.

I took the controller from him and clicked on "start." Immediately, a lion came out of the bush and ate me.

"What happened?" I asked.

"Oh snap! That jankity old lion just busted your grill. You should've ducked and the lion would've jumped over you. It's my turn now."

Jake took the controller from me, and about twenty minutes later, I timidly asked, "Jake?"

"Yeah?" he replied without taking his eyes from the TV screen.

"Do you want to do something else for a while?"

"Are you clowning on me? I've got one more dude to cap before I get to the next level."

"OK," I said, sighing and getting up to wander the room. After another fifteen minutes, I sat down next to him again. "You almost done?"

"Sorry, dude. I forgot you were here. I've never gotten this far on my first guy before," Jake said, continuing to play.

I started hoping with all of my might his dude would die. I was desperate for a way to get him to stop playing the game. I'd walked around his basement so many times I started to feel like all the models' eyes on the posters were following me. I chewed a hangnail.

"How about I ask you a question and then you ask me a question?" I said.

"Whatever."

"Um, all right," I said, reminding myself that he was Jake Harris and I was just Mia Fullerton, I should be grateful that he'd invited me over. "If you could have any job in the world, what would it be?"

"Professional football player."

After five minutes of silence, I finally said, "Um, now you're supposed to ask me something."

He continued staring at the screen.

"Do you think the Chicago Bears' defensive team has a chance against the Vikings' offense?"

"What?"

"Don't you watch football?"

"Not really."

"How whack is that?"

"I watch the WNBA," I offered.

"That's just a bunch of chicks playin' ball." Jake returned his focus to the video game, where an entire fleet of aliens was attacking his dude. I decided to give it one more try.

"Um, if you could live anywhere, where would it be?"

"Ohio."

"Ohio?"

"Duh, the Football Hall of Fame is in Canton, Ohio." Jake threw down his controller and said, "I'm tired of talkin' and my dude just died. Do you wanna watch a movie?"

"Sure. What do you have?" I asked, envisioning a romantic comedy so I could snuggle in his arms.

"How 'bout the first *Robo* movie? It's off the chain. The special effects are the butta."

"Great." *He is Jake Harris, He is Jake Harris, He is Jake Harris* . . . I repeated to myself.

The rest of the evening was spent watching *Robo Destructive Force*, an endless display of people getting mutilated, evaporated, beheaded, or just plain killed. All thoughts of romance disintegrated as I swallowed the bile rising in my throat.

Mercifully, Jake's mom called down the stairs a few minutes later, "Mia, your mom is here."

I jumped off the couch and dashed for the stairs.

"Thanks for a great evening, Jake."

"Aren't you forgettin' something?"

"Oh yeah, my jacket. Thanks for reminding me." I grabbed my jacket off the couch.

"Um, I kinda thought, after how you acted at the movies, that we might . . . you know . . ."

"What?"

"You know."

"No, I don't."

"Come on, you know what I'm talkin' about."

It suddenly occurred to me he wanted me to kiss him.

"Jake, my mom's upstairs. Why didn't you try to kiss me before?"

"I dunno. I guess I was waiting for you."

I did a mental brain slap. How come I always had to make the first move with Jake? Jeez, if Tim were in the basement with me, I doubt I would've had to play video games, watch human mutilation, and make the first move. Tim and I never ran out of things to say to each other. In fact, Tim . . . Then I realized I was doing it again. I was going to kiss Jake while thinking about Tim.

Tim was *not* going to ruin my love life. I pulled my retainer from my mouth and kissed Jake like I had the last time. I figured I knew what I was doing, because Jake wouldn't stop kissing me once we started. Then his tongue started its lizard routine and darted in and out of my mouth. I struggled not to gag.

Jake's mom called again, "Mia? Are you down there?"

"Coming!" I pried my lips from Jake's and hurried up the stairs, wiping his saliva off my chin.

When my mom gave me the fish eye, I knew she was checking for hickeys. Jake ambled up the stairs behind me.

"Thanks for letting Mia hang with me tonight, Mrs. Fullerton."

"You're welcome, and I hope you had a good time." Then, in her best teacher voice, she asked, "Did you finish your English assignment for tomorrow?"

"Uh, not yet. I was just gonna do that."

Jake's mom raised an eyebrow.

"You told me you didn't have any homework tonight."

Not wanting to see Jake get dogged on by his mom, I said, "See you, Jake," and hurried my mom out the door.

"Did you have a nice time?" she asked once we were in the car.

I buckled up. "It was interesting," I mumbled.

Chapter
Thirteen

"**W**here were you this morning?" I asked Lisa as I twirled the combination to my locker. "I stopped by your house so we could walk to school together, but your mom said you'd already left."

Lisa slammed her locker door. "Do I know you?"

"Ha, ha, very funny. I'm sorry I haven't talked to you very much lately, but Jessie and I are so busy planning the dance and getting student council stuff done, I haven't had a chance."

"As long as you have a good excuse."

Judging by her attitude, I decided to change the subject.

"How was Academic Quiz Bowl practice last week?" I asked. "I'm sorry I missed all the practices, but Jessie and I—"

Lisa silenced me with a glare.

"The Academic Quiz Bowl practices were great," she said. "Tim and Mike are really dedicated to the team."

"Meaning I'm not? It's not my fault student council work is taking up all my time."

"Isn't Jessie supposed to help you, or is she too afraid of breaking a nail?"

"Actually, Jessie's pretty cool. I never thought I'd say this, but she's really nice."

"I'm getting worried about you," Lisa said as we headed down the hallway. "It's weird enough you're going out with Jake, but now you're becoming friends with Jessie? If you don't watch it, you're going to become one of them."

"It's not like they're alien invaders, Lisa. They're just people."

"All right, but don't say I didn't warn you." We walked silently to American History class. Finally, Lisa sighed.

"So, have you hired a DJ for the dance yet?" she asked.

Grateful for the reprieve, I said, "Jessie hired some awesome DJ. I guess he's really hard to get. We're lucky he had a cancellation and agreed to do our dance."

"If you need any help on the decorations committee, I'd be glad to volunteer," she said. "I've got some terrific posters of Einstein, and I found some streamers with the theory of relativity stamped on them. We could do a theme of theorems and equations. It would be totally original."

"Thanks, but I think we're going mainstream and doing a fall theme. You know, hay bales, pumpkins, scarecrows . . . Jessie said if we position the hay bales correctly, people can make out behind them."

"Well, I wouldn't want to disagree with Jessie," Lisa said a bit caustically.

I was getting a little tired of Lisa's attitude. After all, Jessie and I had spent hours working on perfecting the details to the dance. Who was she to judge what we had planned? "Anyway," I replied, "who'd want to dance in a gym filled with scientific formulas?"

"I would, and not so long ago, you would have, too."

"Well, now I know better. And I think Jessie and I have a better idea of what the ninth graders want as decorations for their dance than you do. If you remember, they elected us, not you."

"It's amazing how fast this presidential power has gone to your head," Lisa said. "Go plan your own dance with all your new *popular* friends, but don't say I didn't warn you when they drop you and you need a real friend."

"A real friend doesn't judge others when they finally succeed!"

"If you judge success by how popular you are, then we're through being friends."

"My thoughts exactly," I said, storming into Mr. Benson's room and choosing a new seat—next to Jessie.

For Friday's lunch period, Jessie and I rolled into the cafeteria the ancient wooden cart that we used as our student store.

"No wonder they make freshmen push this cart around," she panted. "No upper classmen would be caught dead wheeling this hunk of junk to the cafeteria every day."

"I know, but next week, thank goodness, we can get the other freshmen student council members to start working the store. It's been horrible."

"Tell me about it. Between ordering sweatshirts, planning the dance, and organizing the student council meetings, I haven't had a life the past few weeks," Jessie said, unlocking the cart. "And I know it's been the same for you. That's why I feel so bad about making you work our last shift alone, but my mom is making me keep my dentist appointment. Are you sure you don't want me to find someone else to work with you? What about Lisa?"

"No, thanks," I said. "I'll probably just use the time to work on some homework."

"Yeah, that math test today sounds like it's gonna be tough."

"There's a test today?" I said.

"Don't you remember?" Jessie said. "Grizzling announced it last week. Haven't you studied?" Jessie looked at her watch. "Look, I wish I could help you out, but I've gotta go. My mom's gonna be waiting for me at the office."

She left the cafeteria and I pulled my math book out of my backpack, frantically scanning the chapters. By the time the lunch bell rang, I'd sold fourteen pencils, three erasers, two notebooks, and one set of markers, and still wasn't any closer to learning any math facts.

When I started putting the supplies away, Anthony, running over to the cart, yelled, "Hold up! I need a pencil for Grizzling's class and I'm cashed out. Can you mack one for me?"

I hesitated.

"Well, I'm not supposed to give anything away. I might get in trouble . . ."

Jake walked up beside me and put his arm around my waist.

"Come on, dude, it's just a pencil. You wouldn't leave one of my dawgs hanging, would ya?" Jake looked directly into my eyes, melting all my morals. I handed Anthony a pencil.

"You're right. Here—take one."

"You are da bomb!" Anthony said, grabbing three more pencils and stashing them in his pocket.

"While you're at it, I *really* need some markers for art class. I promise I'll get you some Benjamins later." Collin took a handful of markers and shoved them in his folder.

Jake grabbed a bunch of pens from the bin.

"Dude, your mom makes us write everything in pen, and I don't want her tripping on me, especially since I'll be kicking it with my breezy tonight at the movies."

"We're going to the movies tonight?" I asked, busily trying to add in my head how much money I had to pay back to the store before Mr. Benson noticed a discrepancy in the books.

"For sheezy. Be at the mall at seven."

"Wait—I can't go to the movies with you tonight. I told my parents I'd stay home with Chris because they won't be home until late. If you'd asked earlier, I probably could've figured something out."

"How old's your brother?" Collin asked.

"He's twelve, but they don't trust him to stay by himself at night. My parents are kind of overprotective."

"That's totally whack," Anthony said.

"I guess we'll just have to chill at the dance next week, dude." Jake put the pens in his pocket. "I'll call you later."

I watched Jake and his friends leave and sighed dreamily. I was going to my first high school dance with Jake Harris. It was all too good to be true.

"Earth to Mia," Tim said, pounding a quarter on the counter.

"Sorry, the store's closed. You'll have to come back next week."

"Oh, come on. I need to buy a pencil for Grizzling's class," Tim pleaded.

"Let's make a deal. You help me get caught up for the Academic Quiz Bowl this weekend, and I'll let you buy a pencil."

"Why don't you ask Lisa to help you?"

"That's none of your business," I said, dangling the pencil in front of his face. "If you help me, I'll also make chocolate chip cookies while we study."

"You had to say 'chocolate chip cookies', didn't you? All right, it's a deal. How about tonight?" Tim took the pencil and handed me the quarter.

"My parents are going to be gone, but I'm sure they won't care if we study together. Why don't you come over at seven?"

"I want those cookies warm, right out of the oven," Tim ordered, running out the cafeteria door.

I put the supplies away in their bins, locked up the cart, and slowly rolled it to the doors that led to the courtyard. Holding one door open with my hip, I spread my arms out and pushed the other door open. I heaved the cart through the opening, but wasn't quick enough. I ended up leaving a layer of ankle skin in the doorway.

Now the hard part: how am I going to push this two-ton cart past all these people, up the hill, and into the main building all by myself? I rubbed my ankle and looked at all the students sprawled around the courtyard soaking up the warm fall sun before they headed to their next class.

I started pushing the cart up the hill, panting and wheezing. I felt like the Little Engine That Could and started chanting in my head, *I think I can, I think I can, I think I can . . .*

After the millionth *I think I can*, I finally reached the summit of the hill. Stopping to catch my breath, I was instantly swarmed by a gang of bees, obviously drawn to the sweat dripping down my cheeks. Ever since the TV movie *Killer Bees*, I've been terrified of bees, and these bees definitely looked like veterans of the movie. I swatted at them with both hands, forgetting I was holding onto a cart the size of Alaska. As soon as I let go, the cart started to careen down the hill, like the Little Engine on steroids.

The cart swayed to and fro, gaining momentum with every inch. Students hurled themselves out of the way as the cart plowed through the courtyard and smashed through the plastic orange traffic cones that divided it from the teachers' parking lot. Miraculously, just as my parents' insurance premium was about to hit a record high, the cart lost a wheel, teetered for a second, and then crashed, millimeters from Mrs. Jenson's Hummer.

Pencils, pennants, and papers exploded into the air, flying across the courtyard and into the hands of the greedy masses. I dashed down the hill to the chaos as students swarmed the supplies like a flock of vultures diving onto a newly deceased carcass. It was total mayhem as people grabbed whatever they could, shoving school supplies into their pockets. All would have been lost if Sister Donovan hadn't swooped down like an angel from Heaven and shouted, "What is going on here?"

I came forward meekly. "Um, I crashed the student store."

Sister Donovan sighed. "Mia Fullerton, are you purposely trying to give me a head full of gray hair?"

"Not really."

Sister Donovan turned from me and glared at the students with their pockets full of stolen goods.

"Any student who unlawfully obtained supplies from the student store will serve a week's worth of detention."

A few students guiltily emptied their pockets and dumped supplies onto the courtyard, not making eye contact with Sister

Donovan.

"Remember," said Sister Donovan, staring at the surrounding faces. "Jesus sees everything." More students dropped their stash. A few whispered, "I'm sorry, Sister Donovan," while making the sign of the cross.

"And anyone who is caught will be prosecuted to the fullest extent of the law," she added. Finally, Anthony, Collin, and Jake emptied their pockets.

"That's better. Now, I want you to give Mia some space so she can clean up this mess. I will see that Father Michael visits with all of you in religion class next week to talk about the seventh commandment: 'Thou shall not steal.' And it wouldn't hurt for some of you to visit a confessional."

As everyone shuffled away, I looked at the merchandise, scattered across the playground. Rubbing a hand across my eyes to hide my tears, I started gathering supplies and loading them back into their plastic bins. I wearily picked up a St. Hilary's pennant when Tim knelt down beside me.

"Need any help?"

I threw the pennant into a bin.

"How many cookies is it going to cost me?"

"This favor is free. It's just my good deed for the day." Tim handed me a Kleenex from his pocket.

I eyed it warily.

"It's clean, I promise."

As I blew my nose into it, Tim added, "I mean, I only used it once."

After we deposited the last of the bins into Mr. Benson's room and lugged the cart's remains to the dumpster, I said, "If we hurry, we can still make it to the end of math class."

Tim closed the dumpster lid. "Good thing I'm faster than you."

"In your dreams," I said.

We reached the room just as our classmates were pouring out the door. I ran to Mr. Grizzling's desk. "I'm sorry I missed class, but the student store collapsed in the courtyard and I had to pick up all the supplies. Sister Donovan can verify it for you."

"What's your excuse, Mr. Radford?"

"I was helping her."

"Are you even on student council?"

"No sir, I was just helping."

"A likely story," Mr. Grizzling growled. "As you know, we had a test today. Ms. Fullerton, you will be allowed to take the test after school—after I verify your story with Sister Donovan. Mr. Radford, you will receive a zero, because you do not have a legitimate excuse. But I won't turn you into the office for truancy."

"But I was helping Mia!" Tim said, astounded.

"I think you should thank me instead of standing there sputtering," Mr. Grizzling said.

"But I wouldn't have been able to clean up the mess as fast without Tim," I said.

"Ms. Fullerton, I suggest you hold your tongue."

I put my hands on my hips. "That is so unfair. If Tim can't take the test, then neither should I."

Tim nudged me in the ribs. "What are you doing? You should take the test. You need the points more than I do."

"No way! Either we both get to take the test or neither of us does."

"Ms. Fullerton, I can see you have your mother's fortitude." Mr. Grizzling glowered at me. "Very well, I will allow both of you to take the test after school today. But I highly suggest you never talk to me in that manner ever again."

I silently nodded my head, figuring I shouldn't press my luck with Mr. Grizzling, and Tim and I walked into the hallway. Tim said,

"I can't believe you stood up to him like that for me. What got into you?"

I smiled. "I was just doing my good deed for the day. A friend taught me that."

Chapter
Fourteen

Tim opened the back door to my house. "I smell cookies!"

"Haven't you ever heard of knocking?"

"Knocking's for wimps," Tim said, shoving a cookie in his mouth and grabbing for another one. "I got all my trivia cards. Are you ready?"

"Ready as I'll ever be," I said, plopping onto the family room couch next to Tim. He pulled out the first question.

"Which of the Great Lakes is entirely within the United States?"

"Lake Michigan."

"Who drafted the Declaration of Independence?"

"Thomas Jefferson."

"Who wrote *The Last of the Mohicans*?"

"James Fennimore Cooper. Come on, give me a tough one."

"All right. What's a henway?"

I thought for a moment. "I don't know, what's a henway?"

"About three pounds! Get it? What does a *hen* weigh?" Tim fell off the couch laughing hysterically. "I can't believe you fell for it! That's the oldest joke in the book."

"I guess my humor must be a little more sophisticated than yours. You probably like the Three Stooges."

"Who doesn't like the Three Stooges? They're comic geniuses!" Tim climbed back onto the couch.

"It's genius to poke each other's eyes out and saying 'nyuk, nyuk,

nyuk'?"

"You just don't have a sense of humor," Tim said, shoving another cookie in his mouth.

"I have a great sense of humor!" I said.

"People who aren't funny always say they have a great sense of humor. Just admit it—I'm funnier than you."

"You may be funnier *looking*, but I have a great sense of humor. My family thinks I'm hilarious."

"Why don't we go outside and ask your brother, then? He's playing football with Kevin right now." Tim headed for the door.

"What about our Quiz Bowl practice?" I asked feebly, hoping to keep Tim from finding out I hadn't made my family laugh since learning to speak.

"Trivia can wait. You seem to be doing fine." He yelled out the door, "Hey, Chris, does your family think Mia is funny?"

"I always crack up when I see her," Chris said, tossing the football to Tim.

"Really?"

"Yeah, just look at her face—that's enough to make anyone crack up!"

"Creep!" I ran out the door and tackled Chris.

"Come on, Mia!" Kevin yelled. "Let's you and me take on Tim and Chris in a game."

Tim pounded his fist into the palm of his other hand. "You're on!"

Kevin pulled me over in a huddle and whispered, "You go long and I'll throw it to you. Got it?"

Not having a clue what he meant, I hesitated. "Um, yeah."

"You are toast," Tim taunted as we faced each other across the line of scrimmage.

I ran to the end of the yard, and Kevin threw me a perfect spiral. I had the ball on the tips of my fingers when I was pummeled from behind. Tim grabbed the ball before it hit the ground.

"Interception!"

"I thought this was touch football!" I said, standing up and brushing the grass off my jeans.

"What, you too much of a pansy to play a real man's sport?" Tim asked, strutting around the yard.

"I'll show you who the pansy is," I said. I got into formation, again lining up across from Tim. Tim cut across the field, and Chris threw him the ball hard. I sprinted to keep up, leapt in the air, and tackled Tim as he caught the pass. "Need any help getting up?" I said, offering him a hand.

Tim pushed my hand away and growled, "The game has just begun."

During the next play, I intercepted the ball from Chris and raced it back all the way for a touchdown. Just as I crossed the line, Tim grabbed me from behind and tackled me to the ground, falling right on top of me.

"Too late," I said. "The score counts."

Tim was breathing hard and I stopped smiling, realizing he was still on top of me. We stared at each other for a minute, and then Tim leaned toward me.

"Come on!" Chris yelled. "What are you two doing? Is this football or *The Dating Game*?"

I pushed Tim off me. "All right," I said, "no more football. I've proven my point that I can outplay Tim in any sport he chooses." I walked into the house and went straight to the bathroom to splash cold water on my face—to cool down from both the game and my close encounter with Tim. The phone rang.

"Hey, Tim, would you answer that?" I yelled from the bathroom. "It's probably my parents checking up on us."

After a moment, Tim knocked on the bathroom door. "It's for you. It's Jake."

I hurriedly dried my face and took the phone from Tim's hand. "Hello?"

"What's Tim doin' at your crib?"

I walked into the kitchen for some privacy. "I only invited him over so he could help me study for the Quiz Bowl. Otherwise, I wouldn't go near him. You know I can't stand him."

"It's all good, but he better not be triflin' with my breezy."

"Tim's nothing to me."

"Dude, why don't I come over? We can chill and . . . well, you know . . ."

"No," I said nervously. "That wouldn't be a good idea. I don't know when my parents will be back, and I'd hate to get grounded and miss the dance next Friday."

"I guess we'll have to wait to get busy."

I laughed uneasily. "Um yeah . . . How about I talk to you Monday at school?"

"Holla back. Peace out," he said, hanging up the phone.

I turned around to do the same and bumped into Tim.

"Were you listening in on my conversation?"

"I just came in to get a drink of water, but I couldn't miss a *friend* saying she couldn't stand me. Lisa was right—you *have* turned into a snob. And since you obviously can't stand me and I'm nothing to you, I guess you don't need my help studying. See you later, *dude*." And he slammed the door behind him.

My roller coaster car plunged downward at a terrifying speed. Just as I was about to smash into smithereens, Tim suddenly appeared at the bottom of the hill, wearing a football jersey. "Don't worry," he said. "I'm here to help. That's what friends are for." Then he pulled out some maracas and began singing *Copacabana*.

I bolted upright in bed, covered with sweat, but Barry Manilow continued to croon about Lola and Tony's doomed love affair. I pinched myself to make sure I wasn't hallucinating as Barry concluded his sad story and was replaced by Michael Bolton wailing out a love song. I turned off my alarm clock and yelled, "Chris, stop messing with my radio!" It was bad enough dreaming about Tim, but Tim combined with Barry Manilow and Michael Bolton was just too much for me first thing in the morning.

My mom poked her head in my room.

"Good morning, honey. I can't wait to hear your report on Joan of Arc today."

Oh my God! Is that today? "I totally forgot to get a costume," I stammered. "I've been so busy planning tonight's dance."

"I figured as much. I've been hearing from more than a few teachers that your grades are starting to slip. You know that in this house, school comes first." She picked up some dirty clothes from my floor and threw them into the laundry basket. "Your room could use a little attention, too."

"Is the lecture over so I can get ready for school now?"

"First, though, my surprise. I know how hard you've been working on student council, and since I'm the best mom in the world, I took the liberty of getting you a Joan of Arc costume!" She left my room and came back lugging an enormous suit of armor. "I know you should have made a costume on your own, but I just couldn't help myself when I saw this in the costume shop window! Isn't it great?"

I pulled my jaw up off the floor.

"Uh, 'great' isn't the word that first comes to mind." I crawled out of bed and looked closer at the armor. "Too bad it's dented."

"The dents signify the wounds she received in battle—one to her head and one to her breastplate. You should know that from your research."

"Oh, right. I was just testing to see if you remembered." To tell the truth, I hadn't read anything about Joan of Arc since being grounded. I sighed, "All right, I'll wear it, but can you keep the costume in your room until class time? I don't think it'll fit in my locker."

Mr. Benson met me at the classroom door. "Mia, don't panic."

Not a good way to start a conversation.

"OK, what shouldn't I panic about?"

"I've got some bad news for you. The DJ you hired just called. He has the flu and can't make it tonight."

"Don't panic? The dance is tonight! I have to find Jessie!"

"That's the other bad news. Jessie's mom called this morning, and Jessie's grandfather passed away last night. They're on their way to Indiana, and Jessie will have to miss the dance."

I started chewing my fingernails down to the quick. "What am I going to do?"

Mr. Benson shrugged. "I've heard that Mr. Corrigan, one of the custodians, does a little DJ work on the side. You could ask him if he's available."

I descended the creaky steps to the basement. "Hello? Mr. Corrigan?"

"I'm in the back, by the furnace," a voice called out.

I stepped tentatively between a maze of textbooks and old AV equipment and headed back to the furnace room. Mr. Corrigan looked up as I approached.

"Well, lookee here. Why, if it isn't Maureen Fullerton's little tyke all growed up. I remember when you used to follow me around when you were no bigger than a corn stalk that's knee-high on the Fourth of July. Remember how I used to pull a quarter out of your ear? Or when I used to take your nose and hide it in my hand? How about when I used to make my thumb come off of my hand?" Mr. Corrigan proceeded to pretend to pull his thumb off his hand. I laughed awkwardly.

"Sorry, Mr. Corrigan, I don't remember that."

"I guess you'd be too old to fall for those tricks now. Hey, what's that? Come over here. You got something in your ear." Mr. Corrigan pulled me closer.

"What? Take it out!" I yelled, imagining that a cockroach had emerged from his feast of textbook glue and decided to snack on my earwax.

"Well, lookeee here!" Mr. Corrigan proudly showed me a quarter he had supposedly pulled out of my ear. "I guess the bigger you are, the harder you fall!"

I tried to laugh. "You got me, Mr. Corrigan. The old 'pull a quarter out of the ear' prank—it's an oldie, but a goodie."

"It's one of my fav-o-rites!" Mr. Corrigan whistled. "Now, what can I help you with?"

I took a deep breath and blurted as fast as I could, "Tonight's the ninth grade dance at St. Hilary's and I'm in charge. We hired a DJ, but he got the flu and had to back out. Mr. Benson said you're a DJ on your time off, and I was wondering if you were available to DJ tonight's dance."

"Well, sure, I could do that. The missus and me don't have nothin' else going on tonight. In fact, bein' a DJ for your dance would tickle me as much as a newborn tick on a fat basset hound."

"Um, that would be great, Mr. Corrigan. The dance is at seven in the gym. We'll be there decorating after school today if you want to set up any equipment." I breathed a huge sigh of relief and started heading toward the stairs.

"By the way, what's your theme this year?" he asked.

"We're doing a fall theme. You know—pumpkins, scarecrows, hay bales . . ."

"Super dee duper, I have the perfect music for you. It'll be so good, it'll make you want to slap your granny."

Jake slung his arm around me on the way to English class.

"Dude, I'm barely hangin' onto a C minus and I like totally forgot to get a costume. Will your mom dog on me?"

"Yeah," I answered honestly. "She's pretty strict about stuff like that. Maybe I can help you think of a costume really fast. Who did you write a speech about?"

"Walter Payton."

"Is he an actor or something?"

"Are you clowning on me? Dude, Walter Payton was the best running back in the history of football."

"Well, what would Walter Payton wear?"

"Duh, he'd wear a football uniform."

"So, what do you have in your P.E. locker?" I asked.

"Deodorant?"

I bit my tongue as I prayed for patience. Slowly, I said, "Go get your football uniform out of your locker, and I'll tell my mom you had to run an errand for Mr. Benson."

"You're da' bomb!" Jake called, running down the hallway.

My mom handed me my suit of armor.

"Hurry up and get your costume on. Everyone is already in the restroom getting ready for their speeches."

I took the costume and nearly collapsed under its weight.

"Um, Mr. Benson wanted me to tell you that Jake's running an errand for him, so he'll be a little late."

"Meaning, Jake forgot his costume and you're covering for him?"

"Don't bust him—he really wants to hold on to his C minus."

"I won't bust him this time, but he had better give a good speech. Now, go try on your suit of armor, Joan."

I entered the restroom, dragging my costume behind me.

"Who are you supposed to be?" Cassie asked.

I dropped the suit of armor onto the bathroom floor. "Joan of Arc."

"Good thing you're flat. This cross-dressing thing should really work for you," Cassie replied.

Even though I knew I'd end up regretting it, I said, "What a surprise; you're wearing another cheerleading costume. Originality doesn't seem to be your strong suit, does it, Cassie?"

"For your information, I'm dressed as Paula Abdul. She was, like, the most famous Laker Girl ever. Which I have to say is much better than dressing up as a hallucinating virgin." Then she and Stephanie left the bathroom, their evil laughter echoing behind.

I waited until I had the entire bathroom to myself before opening my costume bag. I pulled out all the pieces of armor and laid them on the bathroom floor. Deciding the gray sweats must go on first, I slid out of my skirt and blouse and climbed into the suit. I had no difficulty with that, so I confidently sized up the rest of the costume.

Figuring the armor leggings would logically go on next, I tried strapping them around my legs, but I couldn't bend over far enough to grab the straps and tighten them onto my calves. Every time I thought I'd fastened the strap, it would unhook and fall off. Finally, I figured out if I sat down on the bathroom floor with my legs extended in front of me, I could stretch out and strap the armor legging onto each of my legs.

"Hey, that wasn't too bad," I said, praising myself as I hooked the last strap.

I started to stand up, but realized my legs were staunchly set straight out in front of me. I couldn't bend them and, considering each legging weighed about twenty pounds, I couldn't even lift my legs off the ground. I was stuck sitting on the bathroom floor with my legs in front of me. If I took off the armor leggings, I'd never get them back on while standing up, so I rolled myself over, thinking I could get up from my hands and knees. But, since I couldn't bend my legs, I just ended up lying face down on the bathroom floor.

"Come on, Mia, what would Joan of Arc do in a situation like this?" Deciding that Joan would be too smart to get stuck on the bathroom floor, I threw my arms up and grabbed hold of the bathroom sink. I slowly hoisted myself up into a standing position. "I knew I could do it," I panted.

Bending over with my legs erect, I lifted up the fifty-pound breastplate harness. When I strapped it around my chest, my knees immediately buckled under the weight, but thankfully I didn't fall. *How in the world did anyone fight in one of these things?*

With sweat dripping down my face and underarms, I strapped on one of the shoulder armors that extended all the way down my arms. Then I grabbed the other shoulder armor. But, since I couldn't bend my arm, I couldn't reach over to fasten the harness on my other shoulder. I finally figured out that if I extended my arm straight out in front of me, and then flapped it using a quick motion, I could gain enough momentum to throw the strap over my arm without having to bend. After fifteen tries, I finally fastened it.

"All right, only the helmet is left," I told myself confidently, panting like a dog on a hot day. I heaved the helmet off the sink and placed it on my head. But the weight of the helmet was so unbearable, my head immediately dropped forward, followed by the rest of my body. I fell, sprawled out on my stomach, stranded on the bathroom floor!

I lifted my visor and yelled, "Help, I've fallen and I can't get up!" No one answered, so I yelled even louder. "Help me, please! I'm on the bathroom floor in a suit of armor and I can't move!" No response, so I screamed at the top of my lungs. "Please help! I see all kinds of hair and other gross things down here and I'm going to be sick!"

Great! No one could hear me. Trying to emulate Joan of Arc's can-do attitude, I tried to unfasten my suit of armor. After several attempts, I knew it was useless. I couldn't bend my arms or legs and the weight of the armor made it feel as if a sumo wrestler was sitting on my back. I was stuck until some unsuspecting soul had to use the bathroom. Then a horrible realization filled my head. I groaned. At this very moment, why did I have to think about using the bathroom?

To occupy my brain with other thoughts, I started counting each and every floor tile, but eventually every thought led back to the fact that if I didn't use the bathroom soon, my mom would have to purchase a very soiled suit of armor. Just as I was about to rust the armor, Lisa peeked her head into the bathroom.

"Mia?"

I almost cried with relief.

"Thank God you're here!"

"Mia, what are doing down there? English class is almost over, so your mom sent me to find you. Have you been down there the whole time?"

"Pretty much—I can't get up, and if I don't go to the bathroom soon, I'll pee my metal pants."

Lisa began laughing so hard that tears started streaming down her face.

"It isn't funny!" I yelled. "Help me up!"

Lisa wiped the tears from her eyes and began unfastening the leg armors.

"Mia, you're the only person I know who can get stranded on the bathroom floor wearing a suit of armor."

"Yeah, I know, I'm hilarious. Now, would you please hurry? I'm dying here!"

The moment she removed the shoulder armor, I ran into a stall.

As I heaved a sigh of relief, Lisa called, "How in the world did you put this on by yourself? These directions from the costume shop say that in medieval times, a squire would assist a knight in putting on his armor. It says here at least one, if not two people, should help someone put on this costume."

"I never was very good at reading directions," I said, coming out of the stall and washing my hands. "Is class really almost over?"

"Yeah, pretty much everyone has given a speech but you," Lisa said.

"How were they? Did I miss any good ones?"

"Tim was Curley from the Three Stooges and he was hilarious!"

I rolled my eyes.

"By the way, who are you supposed to be?"

"Marie Curie, the person who discovered radioactive polonium and radium. She also was the first person to win two Nobel prizes. I, of course, will win at least three."

"I'm sorry I was a jerk and I'm tired of fighting," I blurted out. "What do you say we call a truce?"

Lisa gave me a big hug.

"How can I say no to Joan of Arc?"

Chapter
Fifteen

"What's that awful smell?" I asked no one in particular as I came down the stairs from my bedroom.

My mom walked out of the kitchen.

"Bratwurst and sauerkraut," she said. "Tonight's multi-cultural night, so we're eating German food."

"I can't go to the dance smelling like soggy cabbage!"

My mom gave me an exasperated look.

"Listen, I put a lot of time and research into this meal, so I'm not going to change the entire family's plans just because it doesn't fit into your schedule."

"I didn't complain on Chinese night, when we had to eat with chopsticks while sitting on the floor, or on Mexican night, when we all had to dance with sombreros on our heads, or even on Irish night when Dad sang *Danny Boy* after downing a pint of Guinness, but I'm drawing the line at smelling like a sausage on the most important night of my life."

"We eat as a family," she said, "so sit down and zip it." She placed a pot of German potato salad on the table.

"Are there onions in that?" I asked.

"Lots of them." She smiled as she placed a heaping spoonful onto my plate.

"Hurry up, Mia, it's time to go!" my mom yelled from the bottom of the stairs.

"I'm coming—I'm still trying to get the bratwurst odor out of my hair!" I sprayed a last round of perfume on myself and dashed down the stairs.

My mom pointed at my midriff.

"Pull your shirt down—I can see your stomach."

"You can only see an inch."

"On you, any skin is too much," Chris muttered.

"You're just jealous because you don't get to go to the dance."

"Like I *want* to go to a dance the Freak Queen planned."

The doorbell rang.

"I'll get it—it's probably Lisa."

But when I opened the door, Tim was standing on my front porch.

"What are *you* doing here?" I asked.

"This wasn't my idea," he said. "My parents couldn't take me to the dance, and, before I knew anything about it, asked your parents to drive me." Tim joined Chris on the couch. "By the way, what's that smell?"

"That's just Mia's breath," Chris remarked. "I sure hope Jake likes the smell of sauerkraut."

"Very funny," I said, deciding to brush my teeth one more time, just in case.

Miraculously, we had transformed the gym into an autumn field covered with hay bales and pumpkins. Indian corn graced the concession stand and there was even a scarecrow standing watch in the corner. If we could've lost the sweaty sock odor, everything would've been perfect. I found Mr. Benson at the concession stand.

"Everything looks great," he said, "but we're a little low on candy. You might want to keep an eye on that. Otherwise, I think we should have a profitable dance tonight." He looked up and a scowl formed across his face. "Excuse me, I see some boys switching the signs on the boys' and girls' bathrooms—"

As Mr. Benson dashed off in search of the bathroom bandits, I grabbed Lisa's arm.

"Let's go see how Mr. Corrigan's doing," I suggested.

Lisa followed me to the front of the gym.

"I can't believe Mr. Corrigan is really a DJ. He reminds me of the sort of person who parks his rusted-out Chevy in the front yard and calls it lawn art," she said.

We approached the sound stage and found a woman sitting in a chair, fanning herself with a sheet of paper. She was wearing a fire-engine-red dress so large it easily could have covered a fire truck, and her hair was teased so high, a family of animals might have been living in it.

"Mrs. Corrigan?" I asked hesitantly.

"Who were you expecting? The Queen of England?" Mrs. Corrigan reached down, took off one of her shoes, and began rubbing her foot. "Wooee, my dogs are barking tonight."

"You brought your dogs to the dance?" I asked.

"That's a good one! Mr. Corrigan didn't tell me you were so funny." Mrs. Corrigan looked me over. "Say girl, you're so skinny you'd have to turn around twice to make a shadow. You need some meat on them bones if you ever expect to hitch your wagon to a gravy train."

"Um, have you seen Mr. Corrigan?" I asked, chewing on a hang-nail.

"Just hold your horses—the show's about to begin." Instantly, the lights dimmed and Mr. Corrigan appeared under a spotlight, which was really just Mrs. Corrigan shining a giant flashlight on him. He was wearing a red and white checked shirt, a pair of Wrangler jeans, and a belt buckle with "Bud" stamped on the front glittered under the direct light. As if that weren't enough, he wore a red bandana around his neck and a giant cowboy hat on his head.

"Howdy!" Mr. Corrigan yelled. The gymnasium became as silent as a funeral parlor. "I said, 'Howdy,' partners! Now y'all yell 'howdy' back!"

"Oh my God," I moaned. "Please tell me this isn't happening."

"Dawg gone, this crowd's colder than a well-digger's behind in the Yukon," Mr. Corrigan hollered as fiddle music filled the air. "Well, I'm feelin' finer than a frog hair split four ways, so I guess we'll get this shindig goin'!" I rushed to the sound stage.

"Mr. Corrigan, what are you doing?"

"You said it was a fall dance, so we's gonna have ourselves a gen-u-ine hoedown. Now, don't you go worryin' your pretty little head. The next song I'm gonna play is slicker than snot on a doorknob. It'll get your friends a twitterin' like a June bug in a bug zapper."

To the tune of *Dueling Banjos*, I stumbled to the back of the gym in search of Mr. Benson. I finally found him in the coatroom, trying to organize the sea of coats on the floor.

"Hasn't anyone ever heard of a hanger?" he grumbled.

"Mr. Benson, you'll never believe what Mr. Corrigan is doing out there! He's planning a hoedown, and I don't even know what that means! What should I do?"

"That is the least of our concerns," Mr. Benson said. "We're running out of candy, the ice machine broke, so we're serving warm pop, and the boys have switched the signs on the bathroom so many times that even *I* forget which is the correct restroom. Do you think parents will care if we make the bathrooms unisex tonight?"

"Be serious, Mr. Benson! I'm totally freaking out!"

"Calm down. Go try to explain to Mr. Corrigan this isn't the music usually played at a dance, or for that matter, farther north than Arkansas. Ask him if you can look at his CD collection to see if there's any music high school kids would enjoy. I'm going to organize this room."

I approached the front of the gym, and Mr. Corrigan called into the microphone, "Here's the pretty little filly I was lookin' for!"

I quickly covered the microphone with my hand, and whispered, "Uh, Mr. Corrigan, can you turn the microphone off? I'd like to talk to you."

Mr. Corrigan removed my hand, announcing even louder, "Wooeee, now that we have our star gal, we's goin' to get this shindig goin' with a gen-u-ine square dance. What lucky feller would like to be this Missy's partner?"

I frantically tried grabbing the microphone from his hand.

"Mr. Corrigan, I really don't think–"

"Now, don't be yeller, boys. She's a feisty one!" Mr. Corrigan said, holding the microphone out of my grasp. "Come on, boys. Who's gonna' do-si-do with this little filly?"

I saw my dad come forward out of the crowd and head straight for the stage. *Oh God, the only thing worse than being auctioned off like a heifer would be if my dad was the only one who wanted to dance with me!* As I tried to wrangle out of Mr. Corrigan's iron grip, I heard Tim shout, "I'll be her partner."

"Well, I'll be a gnat's whisker," Mr. Corrigan hollered. "We's got our first pardners. Now, don't be shy. We still need three more couples to make this a gen-u-ine square dance."

Thankfully, Lisa and Mike came forward, followed by Maggie, Kelly, and some guys from our art class. I quickly said a prayer to the saints—I didn't know the patron saint of square dancing. Then, grabbing Tim's hand, I mouthed the words, "Thank you."

Tim met my gaze and smiled.

"You owe me, Mia, and this time, the payback's going to be huge."

After our square dance ended, I convinced Mr. Corrigan to play some dance mixes, and then wearily headed to the back of the gym. Jake intercepted me.

"Yo, nice save on that hillbilly dude."

"I told Jake to rescue you from Farmer Fred," Anthony said. "But he dogged on you, man!"

Jake shoved Anthony.

"Stop capping on me, dude," Jake said. "I got an image to protect. Anyways, Mia's used to people baggin' on her."

"What's that supposed to mean?" I said.

"Chill, dude. I just meant how you used to be called 'Mia the Meek.' Now, when are we gonna get busy?"

Suddenly, Doug Dillard, a member of student council, ran up, grabbed my arm, and dragged me to the concession stand.

"Bad news, Mia," he said.

"I wouldn't know what to do if I heard any good news," I said. "Tell me fast—that'll make it less painful."

"We're out of food."

"How can we be out of food? Didn't we order a ton of candy? I remember voting on how much to order at the last meeting."

"Somehow it got back-ordered, and they only sent what they had in stock. The good news is we'll have ten boxes of candy sent to us in November. Maybe we can give it to the homeless in Thanksgiving packages."

"That's a nice thought, but what are we going to do now?" I replied, trying to calm my rising alarm. *I couldn't believe the school board chose this year to take out all the vending machines for the sake of the students' health.* "All right, I have to think. Where is there junk food in the building?"

"I always see teachers munching on candy when they come out of the teacher's lounge," Doug said.

"Doug, you're brilliant! The teachers' lounge candy machine! Now, how can I raid it?" I began pacing.

"Maybe your mom has a key," he said.

I pulled my mom away from a group of parents.

"Listen, I have a huge favor to ask you. We've run out of candy at the concession stand and I want to raid the teachers' lounge. I promise, we'll pay it back when we get our back-ordered candy."

"I don't know, Mia—"

"Please, Mom," I begged. "I won't ever ask for anything again."

My mom paused, then reluctantly handed me her set of keys.

"The key marked with an L will open the lounge. The key to the vending machine is on top of the cupboards, hidden in a cup. You'll have to climb on the counter and feel around for it. I wouldn't turn on the lights because someone might see you, and if you get caught, don't tell them I had anything to do with this. Good luck." She kissed me on the forehead.

"Thanks, Mom. I owe you one."

"And I won't let you forget it, either," she said.

I ran out of the gym.

"What's your hurry?" Tim asked.

"What are you doing out here? I thought you and Cassie would be groping each other on the dance floor."

"I could say the same thing about you and Jake. Where is he?"

"I have important student council business to do right now," I said.

"Cassie had a nail emergency," Tim said, "so I decided to wait out here in the hall to cool down. Where are you headed?"

"Can you keep a secret?"

"Does a bear pee in the woods?"

"Then come with me," I said, dragging Tim down the hall.

In the dark, the school seemed like a mysterious stranger. It was eerily silent and our footsteps echoed as we crept towards the teachers' lounge. I put my mom's key in the lock and silently turned the knob. When we were safely inside, Tim turned the lights on.

"Turn them off!" I yelled. "I swear, if you had half a brain, your head would be tilted."

"I refuse to enter a battle of wits with you," Tim said as he flipped the lights off. "It's against my morals to attack an unarmed person."

"Just be quiet and help me find the key to the vending machine," I whispered, climbing up on the counter. Tim climbed up after me and started feeling around the top of the cupboard.

"I think I have something," he said.

"Is it the key?"

"No, I think it's a dead mouse."

"Gross!"

"No, I guess not. It looks like an old sock. I wonder how that got up here."

"Keep searching," I commanded, rubbing my hand back and forth on the top of the dusty cupboard. "It would be a lot easier if I could see over the top."

"Aha! Got it!" Tim said, holding the key close to my face so I could see it in the dark. I reached for it.

"Great, hand it to me."

Tim hopped off the counter.

"No way—you'll lose it."

"Give it to me!" I yelled, hopping down beside him.

"Shhh! I found it—I get to open the machine. I've always wanted to do this."

"You've always wanted to open a vending machine?" I said, mocking him, even though I was thinking the same thing. "For the last time, give me the key!"

"Hold on, I almost got it. Shoot, I dropped the key. Can you see it?" Tim asked, feeling around the floor. I crouched down beside him.

"Were your parents cousins?" I said.

Tim stood up and got in my face.

"I swear, Mia, if you make one more wisecrack about how stupid I am, I'm going to . . ."

"You're going to what?"

"I'm going to do this." Tim grabbed me and kissed me hard on the mouth. At first, I tried to get away, but as the kiss softened, I found myself leaning toward him. Our mouths explored each other for a few moments, and I wasn't thinking about anything except how good Tim's mouth felt. His tongue did what it was supposed to do and it seemed as if our mouths were perfect fits for each other. I could have gone on kissing him for hours if Mr. Benson hadn't walked in and flipped on the lights.

"Uh, excuse me," he stammered. "Uh, Mia, your mom said you came in here to get some candy from the machine and I thought I would help you. But I see you already found some, um, help."

I quickly stepped away from Tim.

"Well, um, thanks Mr. Benson. Tim offered to help and then we dropped the key, and—"

"Right, I was just helping Mia find the key," Tim said loudly. "Oh look, Mia. The key's on the floor, and here's your retainer. It must have fallen on the floor, too."

I hastily grabbed my retainer and popped it back in my mouth.

"Well, the problem's solved," Mr. Benson said. "I think we can empty the machine and get back to the dance. We have some hungry teenagers out there." Mr. Benson opened the vending machine and began filling a box.

"Great idea, Mr. Benson," I said, avoiding Tim's eyes.

We returned to the gym, and the sound of square dance music

118

filled my ears. I groaned.

"Oh no, not again!"

Mr. Benson laughed.

"Relax, Mia. The kids are asking for this music. I've never seen anything like it. After every few songs, kids start chanting, 'Square dance, square dance, square dance.' This is the most fun I've ever seen students have at a dance. I think you may have started a craze."

"I hope not." I shuddered, imagining myself in a dress like Mrs. Corrigan's. "I better see how Mr. Corrigan's doing."

"Do you want me to go with you?" Tim asked. I couldn't look at him.

"No, I'd better go by myself."

When I got to the sound stage, Mr. Corrigan mopped his brow with his bandana and hollered, "I'm hotter than a rat in a wool sock, but I haven't had this much fun since my mother-in-law's funeral. This dance is goin' as slick as grass through a goose. Don't you think?"

"Um, I guess," I said.

"Some youngin' named Jake, who's hotter for you than a marshmallow on a stick, asked me to play this song and dedicate it to you," Mr. Corrigan said, putting on a slow song. I turned around and Jake was standing there.

"Do you wanna dance?" Jake asked me.

How could I say no to the guy of my dreams?

After I walked into his arms, we began swaying together on the gym floor. I looked across the room and saw Cassie clinging to Tim, but Tim was staring directly at me. I quickly turned away and held onto Jake even tighter. After all, I would be crazy to choose Tim over Jake. I had everything I'd ever wanted. Didn't I?

Chapter
Sixteen

As my feet pounded the pavement during my Saturday morning run, my head swirled with the events of the night before. After our slow dance, Jake and I ended up behind a hay bale. But as he kissed me, I couldn't wait until I could pry my mouth from his. I mean, what if Mr. Benson found me making out with another guy on the same night? It was almost funny. Here I'd gone almost fifteen years without kissing a single boy, and then ended up kissing two guys—two *gorgeous* guys, I should add—in one night.

I pushed myself to run even faster as I tried to figure things out. Why did I enjoy kissing Tim so much more than Jake? I didn't even like Tim. I had drooled over Jake so many years, I should've been jumping for joy he wanted to kiss me. Maybe it was the spontaneity of Tim's kiss that made me tingle. Or, it could have been the thrill of our mission to steal candy from the teachers. Or, maybe it was just the heat of the moment. All I knew was that Tim's kiss made my knees weak, while Jake's made my stomach queasy.

As I slowed my pace to cool down, I decided I needed to stay as far away from Tim as possible while I figured all this out. After all, I'd been waiting five years for Jake to notice me, and I wasn't going to blow it just because my head started spinning after one kiss with Tim.

I was in the middle of my post-run snack when Chris walked into the kitchen.

"I see it's feeding time at the zoo."

I lobbed an apple at Chris's head just as the phone rang.

"I'll get it," he yelled, lunging for the receiver.

I picked up the mushy apple and was about to hurl it at Chris when he handed me the phone.

"Who is it?" I whispered, covering the mouthpiece.

"It's Tim."

"Tell him I'm not here."

"I just told him you were here! What's your problem?"

"Just tell him I'm busy," I said, shoving the phone back to Chris.

"I swear, Mom and Dad must have dropped you on your head when you were a baby." Chris put the phone to his ear. "Tim, Mia is standing right here doing nothing, but told me to tell you she's busy. I guess she just doesn't want to talk to you."

I grabbed the phone and quickly hung it up.

"You jerk! I'm going to my room. I've lost my appetite."

I slammed my bedroom door and started to pick up the layer of clothes on my floor. It would probably be a good idea if I stayed in for the rest of the weekend. I didn't want to run into Tim when my defenses were so low. Who knows what I'd do?

On Monday morning, I stopped by Jessie's locker.

"I'm sorry about your grandpa," I said.

"Sorry I missed the dance. I heard it was unusual."

"'Unusual' is not the word," Stephanie interrupted. "How about 'a total humiliation'? I heard that Harrison High School students are now calling us 'St. Hillbillies.'"

Jessie rolled her eyes.

"I talked to Mr. Benson this morning," Jessie said, "and he told me student council made a ton of money. Mr. Corrigan didn't even charge us for being a DJ, so we had almost no expenses. We made more money in one night than they made all last year. Besides, Cassie, didn't you tell me you and Tim had an awesome time together?"

"You and Tim are the absolute cutest couple," Stephanie added.

I wanted to ask Cassie if Tim had kissed her, too, but I bit my overused lips. Instead, I said goodbye to Jessie and walked into Mr. Benson's room, taking the long way around the back to avoid Tim's desk.

"I have a surprise for you," my mom told the class.

"We're all getting A's on our report cards?" Collin yelled from the back of the room.

"Nice try, Collin," my mom replied. "Since you all did such a great job on your hero speeches, I thought we could squeeze in one more fun assignment before we start our next unit on poetry."

"That's more like a cruel joke," Anthony moaned. My mom silenced him with a look.

"For your next assignment, you'll research a classmate by interviewing the classmate, as well as his or her family and friends. Then, you'll give a presentation on their life to the class. This will be due in two weeks, and to ensure that you don't choose a friend, you'll draw names out of a hat. Who would like to start?"

No one volunteered so—of course—my mom looked at me.

"Mia, why don't you draw first?"

Why did I have to be the teacher's kid? I climbed out of my desk and walked to the front of the room. I reached my hand into the hat, took one look at the name on the paper, and folded it up to put it back.

"No way, Mia," my mom said. "That's against the rules. Whom did you pick?"

I sighed. "Cassie Foster."

After the rest of the class had been paired up, we sat down with our subjects to begin our interviews. Needing a good grade to make up for my Joan of Arc fiasco, I swallowed my pride and said, "So Cassie, would you like to interview me first or should I interview you?"

Cassie lowered her voice.

"Let's make one thing clear—I know you don't like me and I don't like you. Also, you can interview me or my friends, but I don't want you to go near my family. If you do, I'll make you wish you were never born."

"Why? What's the big deal about your family?"

"My parents are extremely busy, important people and they don't have time to talk to a loser like you."

"All right," I said, "but I need an A on this project, so you'd better give me a great interview."

"Everything I do is great," Cassie said.

Thankfully, during science class, we were assigned to take notes from our book. I had successfully avoided Tim since our kiss, which wasn't easy, considering he lived fifty feet from my house. But I was determined to keep my distance from him—at least until the acrobats in my stomach stopped doing cartwheels every time I saw him.

I immersed myself in a paragraph about the lifespan of a fruit fly, trying to ignore Tim's nearness, when a note suddenly appeared on my book. It read: "We need to talk."

I swallowed, trying to make my heart disappear from my throat. I scribbled back a note, which I scooted to Tim. "About what?"

When he looked at me, I feigned innocence. "You know," he wrote.

"No, I don't," I scrawled. "Quit bothering me, I need to raise all my grades!"

"We need to talk about the teacher's lounge."

By now, Jake and Cassie were watching us. "Anything that happened in there will never be discussed again," I wrote. "It was a mistake."

Tim crumpled my response, opened his textbook, and began taking notes furiously.

Ms. Jackson was pacing in her room when we arrived for Quiz Bowl practice.

"As you know, we are only one month away from the competition. We need to get prepared. First of all, we need a team captain. Do we have any volunteers?"

"I nominate Lisa," I said.

"I second the nomination," Mike shouted.

"I'll third it," Tim agreed.

"Good," Ms. Jackson continued. "As you know, the competition is a single elimination tournament, so if we lose a single round, we're finished. The moderator will ask eighteen questions in each round. Each individual team member will be asked two questions, except for the team captains. The team captains will be asked three questions. Questions will be asked in rotation to the two teams and to contestants within the team. Correct answers are worth ten points, with no deduction for incorrect answers. If an incorrect answer is given, though, an individual on the other team may answer it and receive ten points for the team. No teammate assistance may be offered or received on these questions. Answers must be stated within ten seconds after the question is read."

"What if I get a math question?" I interrupted. "I thought I was on the team to answer questions about books or grammar."

"That's a good point. You'll be able to answer all the questions that come to you individually, I hope, but where your language arts experience will be helpful is in the bonus questions. After every third question answered correctly, the moderator will read aloud the bonus question and the team that answered the toss-up question correctly is allowed to discuss the answer. Lisa, as captain, will be the only one allowed to give the answer. If it's correct, you'll receive an additional fifteen points."

"How long does the tournament usually last?" Tim asked.

"The tournament will be all day, so make sure you clear your calendar for the first Saturday in November."

"Are you kidding?" Lisa said. "I've had that date cleared since they announced it last year. My parents are even skipping a wedding of one of their cousins' kids for this."

Ms. Jackson got out the trivia cards.

"You all have one month to live, eat, sleep, and breathe trivia!"

My mom took a sip of her coffee and asked, "Who wrote, 'He gives his harness bells a shake/To ask if there is some mistake./The only other sound's the sweep/Of easy wind and downy flake.'?"

"Robert Frost." I sighed. "All right, that's enough. My teachers have been quizzing me all week and I'm exhausted. I swear, if I hear one more trivia question, I'm going to scream."

My dad walked into the kitchen.

"When Einstein made his famous comment, 'God does not play dice with the universe,' he was expressing doubts about what theory of matter?"

"AAAAAAHHHHH!" I grabbed a piece of peanut butter toast, snatched my backpack off the floor, and ran out the back door.

"So, are you up for some trivia this weekend?" Lisa asked, falling into step beside me.

"No more trivia—I need a break."

"You can have a break after the tournament. Come on, you know how important this is to me."

"What do I have to do?" I asked, defeated.

"I was thinking we could have a Trivial Pursuit tournament tomorrow," Lisa replied, excitedly. "My mom is having some colleagues over to discuss Jungian and existential philosophies, so can we have it at your house?"

"Do I have to invite Tim?"

"Of course you have to invite him—he's on the team. By the way, it's been totally obvious you've been trying to avoid him this week. What's he done now?"

"He just gets on my nerves," I said. It had been almost a week, and I still hadn't told Lisa about the kiss. I hadn't figured things out, and I wasn't ready to hear Lisa's psychological evaluation of the event.

"I think you like him," she said.

"Get real, Lisa, I can't stand him!"

"Love and hate are similar emotions. It takes a lot of passion to hate somebody the way you claim to hate Tim."

"Aw, shut up and let's get to school," I said, running ahead of her.

126

By Saturday afternoon, we had eaten two large pizzas, drank a twelve pack of pop, consumed three bags of chips and a large bag of M&M's, and played seven games of Trivial Pursuit.

Mike picked up a card and smiled as he read, "How do you make a Kleenex dance?"

"It doesn't say that," Lisa yelled, trying to grab the card from his hand.

"I know this one!" Tim shouted. "Put a little boogie in it!"

"Gross!" I screamed.

"I've got a good one," Lisa exclaimed. "Why did the quantum chicken cross the road?"

"Why?" I asked, already beginning to laugh.

"Because it was already on both sides of the road!" Lisa collapsed on the floor with laughter.

I threw a couch cushion at her.

"That doesn't make sense," I said.

Lisa threw the pillows back at me.

"Yes it does, and it's hilarious!"

"Why didn't the cheetah go on vacation?" Tim asked.

"Why?" we all screamed.

"Because it couldn't find the right spot!"

I started throwing pillows at Tim now.

"That's the worst joke I've ever heard!" I said.

"Pillow war!" Tim shouted, hitting me over the head with a cushion.

Lisa and I grabbed pillows and pummeled Mike and Tim while they led a counter-attack.

My mom poked her head into the living room. "It's after five o'clock, guys. I think you've had enough trivia for today. Time to go home and detox your bodies."

"Is it really that late?" Lisa said, jumping up. "I have to get home so I don't miss my mom's guest speaker on Socratic thinking. I hate to leave this big mess and run. Do you mind, Mia? I promised Mike he could hear it, too."

"I can help Mia clean up," Tim offered.

"Great. Let's get going, Mike, I'd hate for you to miss any of it," Lisa said, pulling Mike out of the house.

"Man, that guy is whipped." Tim shook his head. "*Socratic thinking?*"

"I think it's sweet Mike will do anything for Lisa." I piled pizza boxes into a trash bag and made sure to keep my distance from Tim.

"If you really thought it was 'sweet,' you'd be dating Mike. Face it, Mia, you like a guy who challenges you." Tim shoved paper plates into the bag.

"How do *you* know what I like?" I asked, following him out the back door and tossing the bags into the trash bins by the garage.

Tim grabbed my arm and turned me towards him.

"I know you liked our kiss last Friday night."

"That kiss was a mistake. I'm dating Jake, you're dating Cassie, and that's that." I pulled away, not trusting myself in Tim's arms.

"I'm not dating Cassie. I'm just hanging out with her until you get it through your thick skull that *I'm* right for *you*—not Jake. If you want, I'll break up with her tonight."

"Is that so?"

We both whirled around to see Cassie standing behind us, hands on her hips and eyes blazing.

"Cassie!" Tim said in a strangled voice. "What are you doing here?"

"You invited me over to watch DVDs tonight. Remember?" Cassie spat. "I showed up at your house and your mom told me you were over here. So, I came over to rescue you from having to spend any more time with Mia. But I guess I was wrong, and you actually *like* spending time with the Freak Queen. I can't believe you're two-timing me. Don't you know who I am?"

"Cassie, I'm sorry," Tim sputtered.

She held up her hand. "Save it for someone who cares." Then Cassie got in my face. "No one makes a fool out of Cassie Foster. Just remember, Mia the Meek—revenge is sweet."

Chapter
Seventeen

By Friday afternoon, I was desperate. My presentation on
Cassie was due in three days and she hadn't spoken a word
to me since finding out about me and Tim. She'd also sworn
Stephanie and Jessie to silence, so I had no one to talk to and nothing to write about. If I had to repeat my own mom's class during the
summer, I would be the laughing stock of St. Hilary's. I had to get an
A on this assignment—I didn't care about my promise not to speak
to her parents. She'd insisted on it, then made the decision to not
talk to me herself, so I had no other choice. Her parents couldn't
be *that* busy.

After school, I looked up Cassie's address in the phone book. I
rode my bike over to her house and, as I pedaled into her neighborhood, I was shocked. I'd always assumed Cassie was such a snob
because she was rich, but her house was located in the older part of
town where most of the houses were small and broken down. Parking my bike in her driveway, I couldn't believe the condition of her
house. The grass was high, her screen porch was ripped, and rusty
tools were scattered all over the lawn. Walking up to the front door,
I didn't see a doorbell, so I tentatively opened the screen door and
knocked.

"We don't want any!" a voice shouted.

"I'm not selling anything," I called back. "My name is Mia Fullerton and I go to school with your daughter, Cassie."

A man opened the door. His blue eyes and white-blonde hair

were an exact match of Cassie's, but the similarities ended there. While Cassie was meticulous about her appearance, this man was a shambles. He was wearing an old, stained undershirt and ripped jeans, and smelled like he hadn't showered in days. He took a swig of beer from a bottle and asked, "What do you want?"

"I was assigned to interview Cassie and her family for English class. May I come in and ask you a few questions?"

"I don't know why I send Cassie to that hole of a school—I should've put a stop to that Catholic crap a long time ago." Mr. Foster slammed the screen door in my face. "Cindy! There's someone to see you!"

A slender woman came hurrying down the hall and opened the door.

"Can I help you?"

"Um, my name is Mia Fullerton and I was assigned to interview Cassie's family for English class. May I ask you a few questions about Cassie?"

Mrs. Foster opened the door and let me in. Then, flashing a worried expression at her husband, she said, "Why don't we go into the kitchen? I'm sure we'll be more comfortable in there."

I followed her into a surprisingly clean kitchen. Mrs. Foster offered me a glass of lemonade.

"You'll have to pardon my husband. He hasn't been himself since getting laid off last year. He tried to find another job, but gave up after six months. I just can't seem to get him off the couch any more." With a sad look in her eye, she bit her lip as if she might have said too much, and quickly changed the subject.

"Your name is Mia? Cassie's never mentioned you. Of course, I don't get to see her friends very much any more. She's a little embarrassed about the condition of our house. It needs some repair work, but working two jobs, I don't have much time. In fact, you just caught me between my jobs. I really have to get going soon so I won't be late. What would you like to know?"

"I just need some general information about her childhood. You know, where she lived, what she liked to do—that kind of stuff."

Mr. Foster came into the kitchen and grabbed another beer from the refrigerator. "I'll tell you about Cassie. She's a show-off. I remember when the office called because she told them I was on an FBI mission and wouldn't be able to come to parents' night. I was working for the city's maintenance department then. Of course, that's just an uppity way of saying 'garbage man.' Man, can that girl lie." Mr. Foster shook his head as he walked out of the kitchen.

"So, let's get started," Mrs. Foster said crisply, acting as if Mr. Foster didn't exist. "Cassie was born here in Des Moines, and we've lived here in this house since she was a baby."

"Does Cassie have any siblings?"

"No, we were only blessed with Cassie. She made up for it, though. She was a fireball when she was little—always getting into something." Mrs. Foster smiled at the memory. I continued taking notes.

"What are her interests—besides cheerleading?"

"I guess I don't know what she does in her free time. I don't get to talk to her as much as I'd like nowadays because I always seem to be working. I want to make sure she has the money to do all the things her friends do—you know, new clothes, movies, and that sort of stuff. I'm afraid you'd have to ask her what her hobbies are."

The front door slammed and Cassie's voice thundered through the house. "Mom, whose bike is that in the driveway?"

"We're in here, Cassie," Mrs. Foster called. "I have a friend of yours here."

"Who is it?" Cassie asked suspiciously, walking into the kitchen. When she saw me, she stopped. "What is she doing here?"

"I can explain," I said, standing up. "You wouldn't speak to me at school, so I had to find out some information about you some-how."

"Get out of here, now."

"Cassie, that's no way to talk to your friend—"

Cassie stamped her foot and pointed at the door. "She is *not* my friend, and I said get out!"

I spent the rest of the weekend avoiding my biography of Cassie. What was I supposed to write? I couldn't very well tell everyone she lived in a dump, her dad was a drunk, and her mom didn't have time to pay attention to her.

On Sunday morning, a babysitting job was offered to me, and I readily agreed so I could put off my assignment for a few more hours. I got home late Sunday afternoon with a pocket full of cash and a resounding headache from babysitting three kids under the age of six. I found Chris lying on the couch, reading a comic book. I plopped down beside him.

"Where are Mom and Dad?"

"Shopping," said Chris, continuing to read. "Where've you been?"

"Babysitting," I said, flipping on the TV. "What've you done all day, besides sit on your bum?"

Chris put down his comic book. "For your information, I spent the afternoon with the hottest babe at St. Hilary's."

"Yeah, right. Who's that?" I flipped off the TV when I realized nothing was on but football.

"Cassie Foster."

"Cassie was here?"

"Yeah, she said she was supposed to write a report for English class on your most embarrassing moments. Luckily, you've had so many horribly humiliating experiences, it was easy for me to help her. When I showed her those pictures of you with your geeky glasses, braces, and that goofy haircut you got a few years ago, she laughed so hard."

I grabbed Chris's shirt at the collar. "What did you tell her?"

"Lay off," said Chris, pulling away from me. "I just told her about the time last summer when we went swimming and your bikini top fell off at the pool, and no one even noticed! Oh, and I told her about the time you farted in church so loudly the priest lost his place in his sermon. And of course, I told her about the time when you were five years old and the camera crew caught you picking your nose at a Drake basketball game, and then ran the footage on the five, six, and ten o'clock news. I even gave Cassie the video of that one!"

"Oh my God, I'm ruined! How could you do this to me?"

"What? She said it was going to be funny and you knew all about it."

"Do you really think Mom would assign us something that would humiliate each other? My God, Mom's so into peace, love, and kindness, she sometimes thinks Barney is too harsh!"

Chris paused, then said uncomfortably, "So, I guess Cassie lied to me?"

"Ding! Ding! Ding! You win the prize for idiot of the year!" I screamed as I ran up to my room. I slammed my door, sat down at my desk, whipped out a piece of paper, and muttered, "Cassie's not the only one who can play dirty."

On Monday morning, Jake leaned against my locker. "Where've you been all weekend, dude?"

I pulled out my American History textbook. "I babysat, did homework, and studied trivia."

"Dude, I've never met a chick who works as much as you. First, you're doin' student council crap, then it's your grades, now it's the freakin' Quiz Bowl. When are you gonna chill and let loose?"

I smiled at him. "You're absolutely right. I think I'll start chilling in English class today."

"I'm so excited to hear your presentations!" my mom said, beaming. "Who would you like to go first?"

Cassie raised her hand. "Mrs. Fullerton, can I go first?" she asked sweetly.

"Sure, Cassie, I love your enthusiasm," my mom said. "By the way, I was wondering why you never interviewed Mr. Fullerton or me for this assignment."

"I stopped by on Sunday and no one was home except for your son, Chris. He gave me an extensive interview on Mia."

"You based your presentation on an interview with Chris? Hmmm, this should be interesting." My mom gave me a worried look and I slunk down in my seat.

"I need to go to the hallway and get something first," Cassie said. When she returned, she was carrying a poster-size picture of me taken back in sixth grade. I was wearing my pop-bottle glasses, braces, and my favorite boy band T-shirt. My hair was growing out of an ill-advised shag cut I'd received at a beauty school.

To be honest, the shag cut had been popular back then and did look good on small, giggly, blue-eyed girls with blonde hair. Unfortunately, I have straight brown hair and brown eyes, and have never giggled in my life, so it didn't quite work for me. My mom, always trying to save money, dragged me to a beauty school for my new shag hair-do. "Mia, stop worrying," she'd told me. "These are trained beauty school students. They're almost as professional as the beauticians in those fancy-schmancy places you like so much."

Unfortunately, the lady who cut my hair must have been in the remedial class, because I came out looking like someone had taken a weed whacker to my head. It was so bad my mom had to whisk me off to a "fancy-schmancy" shop to repair the damage. The poor beautician did the best she could, but by the time she was finished, most of my hair had ended up on the floor. When this picture was taken, the photographer asked my teacher if I'd lost my hair as a result of some incurable disease.

Cassie propped the picture up on an easel and Anthony whistled.

"Man," he said, "it looks like Mia got hit with the ugly stick right before she had this picture taken!"

"Quiet down, Anthony," my mom warned. "Remember, Mia is my daughter, and I think she looks sweet. Cassie, you may continue with your presentation."

"Thank you, Mrs. Fullerton." Turning to the class, Cassie began, "Many of us feel as if we know Mia Fullerton. Her nicknames include 'Mia the Meek,' 'Mia the Queen of the Freaks,' 'Mia the Class President,' and a few people could call her 'Mia the Make-Out Artist.'"

My mom crooked her eyebrow at that one, and I slunk even farther down in my seat.

"But, even I was amazed at how little I really knew about Mia. For example, did you know that Mia flunked pre-school?"

"I did not," I muttered under my breath. "I just started pre-school early, so I had to go an extra year."

"Mia also received speech therapy when she was younger because she had a nasty lisp," Cassie continued. "That's why she never spoke in kindergarten—it wasn't that she was shy, it was that Mithess Jonesth wasth justh too hard for her to thay," she lisped.

"Cassie, I don't think that is approp—" my mom began.

"It's all right, Mom," I said. "I did have a lisp. Let her go on." This was going to be humiliating enough without my mom defending me. It was better to just sit and take it. I was going to get my turn next. As Cassie said, revenge is sweet.

Cassie's speech went on for over five minutes—she'd definitely done her research. Even I'd forgotten some of the incidents she recited for the class. Cassie ended her speech with the infamous nose picking video, pausing it on a clip of my face with my finger fully extended up my nose.

The class sat in stunned silence for a minute.

"Dude, that was so cold," Anthony said finally, "I think it's gonna snow in here."

"Man, Cassie, what did Mia ever do to you?" Collin asked.

"I was just following Mrs. Fullerton's directions," Cassie said innocently. "She said to interview family and friends, and then give an accurate portrayal of a classmate."

"I hardly think that was accurate," Lisa objected.

"You could have interviewed me for a more correct assessment," my mom said at the same time.

I spoke loudly over both of them.

"Thanks for that presentation, Cassie. But, I think we've heard enough about me. Why don't you sit down and let me talk about you for a while?" I climbed out of my seat and stood in the front of the room.

"Cassie Foster is not who she says she is, either."

I paused for dramatic effect and looked at Cassie. Did I see a flicker of fear in her eyes? I started again.

"Cassie has tricked everyone into thinking she leads the perfect life, but, in truth, her life is not what she says it is."

Locking eyes with Cassie, I sensed the undeniable aura of dread surrounding her. With my speech, I had the power to destroy all the illusions people had about her. I could be the one to finally bring her down. I lowered my eyes and saw her hands clutched into fists. I knew from experience she was clamping them together to keep them from shaking.

Without warning, a quote I read in one of my thousands of trivia books abruptly popped into my head: "You can discover what your enemy fears most by observing the means *he* uses to frighten you."

Cassie had spent her entire life making fun of me. Could that mean she was actually afraid of me—Mia the Meek? Cassie's lips trembled, waiting for me to continue telling the class about her dysfunctional family. But I knew I didn't have it in me to ruin another person's life. My life wasn't perfect, but at least I had a dad who loved me and a mom who knew what I did in my free time. I even had a little brother who cared enough about me to remember all my humiliating experiences. What more could anyone ask for?

I quickly improvised.

"Cassie's life isn't what she says it is because her dad was once an FBI agent. He worked on all the top secret cases, but in the end, he gave up his promising career to stay at home with Cassie . . ."

Cassie was waiting for me in the hallway after English class.

"I bet you think you're so much better than me now," she said.

"Can't we just end this fight?" I asked.

"One of these days, Mia the Freak, Jake will find out who you really are, and then he'll come running back to me."

"Relying on my leftovers now?" I said. "My, how the mighty have fallen. Why don't you get a life and leave mine alone?"

I left Cassie standing alone in the hall.

Chapter
Eighteen

After a tortuous month of trivia tedium, the Friday afternoon before the Quiz Bowl finally arrived. I only had to survive math class, and then I could focus all my energy on winning. Mercifully, the bell finally rang and I jumped out of my desk.

"Ms. Fullerton," Mr. Grizzling said as I made a break for the door, "I would like a word with you."

"Yes, sir?" I hung back hesitantly while my classmates emptied the room.

"Your mother tells me you're nervous about the math questions at tomorrow's tournament."

"Yes, sir." *Couldn't my mom keep anything secret?*

"While math may not be your strongest subject, I believe it is your timidity in the subject that is holding you back, not lack of aptitude. If you think you can succeed, then half the battle will be won."

"Yes, sir." I was beginning to sound like a parrot.

"Good luck tomorrow, Ms. Fullerton." Mr. Grizzling extended his hand and I shook it. Maybe there really were such things as miracles.

"I have just been informed that there will be sixty-four teams competing tomorrow," Ms. Jackson said. Tim pretended to shoot a basketball.

"Just like March Madness," he said. "We're going to the Big Dance."

"Sweet Sixteen, here we come," I said, rebounding the imaginary ball and pretending to dribble it around the room.

"We're headed to the Final Four," said Mike, swooshing the ball into an imaginary net.

"Where we'll win a touchdown!" Lisa said excitedly.

We dropped our imaginary balls and looked at her.

"What?" she asked. "Isn't that what you need to win in basket-ball?"

Ms. Jackson shook her head. "As I was saying before I was rudely interrupted by your basketball metaphors, there are sixty-four teams, and there will be six rounds of competition. Each round starts at the top of the hour, with an hour break for lunch. Round one begins at nine a.m., so we should meet at school at eight tomorrow morning. I'll drive you all to the competition, so don't be late."

My mom shook me awake.

"Mia, get up! Its seven forty-five. We all overslept!"

I couldn't believe it. The one night I wanted my roller coaster to crash me awake, it hadn't. I jumped out of bed and after a frantic, chaotic rush to get ready, I hurled my body into St. Hilary's at eight fifteen to find Lisa waiting at my locker, impatiently checking her watch.

"Where were you? We're late!"

"I'm sorry. Just let me get my folder from my locker and I'll meet you at Ms. Jackson's car."

"All right, just hurry! Our first round is in forty-five minutes."

I opened my locker and rummaged around, trying to find my folder. After emptying the contents of the locker onto the floor, I finally found it under my gym clothes. Quickly throwing the rest of my books back inside, I slammed the locker door and turned to leave, but I saw something gleaming on the floor in front of my locker, and bent down to pick it up. It was the laminated quadratic formula Mr. Grizzling had given me. I was about to shove it back in my locker when Lisa shouted at me from down the hall.

"Come on, Mia! Ms. Jackson is waiting!"

I hastily put the formula in my pocket and raced after Lisa. "I'm coming!" I yelled.

When we entered the classroom for the first round, Ms. Jackson joined our parents in the back of the room. In the front of the classroom, there were two rows of four desks facing each other. Between the rows, there were two desks facing forward, where the moderator and the timekeeper would sit. The team from Grant High School was already seated on one side, so we took the seats on the other side and waited for the moderator to arrive. Soon, a tall woman and a man resembling a Keebler elf entered the room.

"Good morning," the woman said, "and welcome to the first round of the Academic Quiz Bowl. My name is Mrs. Turner, and this is Mr. Potts. In this round, I will be reading the questions and Mr. Potts will be the timekeeper. I believe you know the rules, but I will remind you that you must answer the questions within ten seconds, and the team captain must give the answer for all bonus questions."

Both teams sat silently, fearing that if either of us made a sound, it would be held against us.

"Team captains, please come forward and draw a number to see who will begin the round," Mrs. Turner instructed.

Lisa and the team captain from Grant drew numbers from a bowl and handed them to Mrs. Turner.

"St. Hilary's will go first in this round," she said.

Lisa smiled broadly and sat down. Mrs. Turner pulled the first trivia card.

"Identify the command used in BASIC to tell the computer to jump to the specified statement number."

"GOTO," Lisa answered quickly.

"Correct. Ten points awarded to St. Hilary's." Mrs. Turner addressed the Grant team next. "Complete these lines taken from Martin Luther King's tombstone: 'Free at last/free at last/thank God almighty . . .'"

"I'm free at last," Grant's captain answered calmly.

"Ten points awarded to Grant High School."

Mrs. Turner looked at Mike. "On which continent would you find the world's largest tropical rain forest and the world's driest place?"

"Um, Africa?"

"Incorrect. Any Grant team member may now answer this question for an additional ten points."

A player from Grant hit her buzzer.

"South America," she answered confidently.

"Correct. Ten more points awarded to the Grant team. Since that was the third question answered correctly, it has a bonus question attached. Your team may confer on this question to arrive at the correct answer. The bonus question is: what two states were created entirely out of other states?"

"Maine and Virginia," Grant's captain answered after his team had conferred.

"I'm sorry, but the correct answer is Maine, from Massachusetts, and West Virginia, split off from Virginia. No bonus points are awarded. The score is St. Hilary's ten points, Grant twenty points. The question returns to Grant High School's second team member. Your question is: Hemingway chose a verse from *Ecclesiastes* as the title of which of his novels?"

"A Farewell to Arms."

"Incorrect. St. Hilary's has a chance to steal."

I hit my buzzer.

"The Sun Also Rises," I said.

"Correct. St. Hilary's and Grant each have twenty points."

The rest of the round went swiftly. Every question was answered correctly, including the bonus questions. Lisa answered the seventeenth question correctly, which gave St. Hilary's a score of 145 points. If the Grant team answered the eighteenth and final question correctly, it would have a chance at the last bonus question. If they answered that one correctly, the team from Grant High School would win. If they made any mistake, *we* would win.

"What percentage of the House of Representatives is elected every two years?"

"One hundred percent," Grant's captain answered, smiling confidently.

"Correct. The final bonus question is: since light cannot escape, how are black holes detected?"

A Grant student hit his buzzer and yelled, "Radio or X-ray astronomy!"

"I'm so sorry," Mrs. Turner reminded him, "but you must let your team captain answer all bonus questions. I cannot give you the bonus points. St. Hilary's advances to the second round!"

We jumped out of our seats and hugged each other. Our parents came over to congratulate us.

"Very nice, students," Ms. Jackson said, "but you're just at the beginning of the day. Don't congratulate each other too much just yet. You need to hustle over to classroom 213 for your next round against Moore High School."

By lunchtime, we'd made it past round three and into the Sweet Sixteen! We were so excited we could barely eat the lunch the competition had provided.

"You need to eat for brain power," Ms. Jackson chided.

"I can't stand this healthy stuff they packed for us," Tim commented, looking in his lunch bag. "Does anybody have any money for the vending machine? I need some junk food."

I reached into my pocket for some money and pulled out my quadratic formula instead.

"I totally forgot I put this in my pocket. Maybe it's a sign from Mr. Grizzling."

"If you mention his name again," Tim groaned, "I won't be hungry for junk food."

I studied the card a little closer. "What does this formula even mean?"

"If I tell you," Tim said, "will you give me five dollars?"

"If you can actually make this formula make any sense to me," I said, "the money is yours."

Tim pulled out a pen and started writing on the napkin from his lunch bag. "First of all, you need to understand the term 'quadratic formula.' To do that, you must understand what is meant by the terms 'quadratic expression' and 'quadratic equation.' A quadratic expression is a polynomial of this form," Tim said, writing $ax^2 + bx + c$ on the napkin. I frowned and concentrated even harder as he continued.

"A quadratic equation is an equation of the form: $ax^2 + bx + c = 0$. Examples of quadratic equations would be: $0 = 6x^2 + 2x + 9$ or $0 = 3.2x^2 + 8.2x - 1.6$. When equations of this form are solved for x, you get the quadratic formula." Tim showed me the card. "That is, you can use this calculation to find the values of x that make the quadratic equation equal to zero. These specific values of x are called the roots of the quadratic equation. They are also called the zeros of the—"

I put my hand over Tim's mouth.

"I'll give you the five dollars if you shut up and never mention this subject again."

"You got it!" Tim yelled, grabbing the five from my hand.

As the rounds progressed, the classrooms became more crowded. Teams who had already lost stayed around, wanting to see who would come out on top. We easily beat Jefferson High School in round four and the Sioux City team in round five. We were going to the championship round!

"We did it!" I yelled, hugging Lisa.

"Not yet," Lisa warned. "We still have to win this round for the championship. Nobody ever remembers the team that gets second place."

When we entered the auditorium for the final round, it was already packed with spectators. The desks for the contending teams had been placed on the stage, so everyone in the audience could see the competition. I climbed the steps to the stage apprehensively and took my seat. Looking down, I saw my parents in the front row, sitting with Ms. Jackson. Then I made the mistake of looking past the front row, where I saw hundreds of high school students from across the state. I gnawed nervously on a hangnail.

Tim looked over at me and grabbed my hand, giving it a squeeze. "We can do this," he whispered in my ear. "We make a great team."

The acrobats started doing cartwheels in my stomach again, which I decided wasn't such a bad feeling. I squeezed Tim's hand back before letting it go.

A man wearing a suit walked up to the microphone. "Welcome to the final round of the Academic Quiz Bowl!"

The crowd broke into thunderous applause and the moderator held up his hands to quiet it.

"My name is Mr. Tibbets and I would like to commend the two teams who made it to the final round: St. Hilary's High School from Des Moines, and Garfield High School from Cedar Falls!"

Mr. Tibbets waited for the applause to die down before he spoke again. "The coaches drew numbers prior to the competition and Garfield High School will begin this round."

There were two other moderators and two timekeepers. They took their places and the competition began.

Coming into the sixteenth question, the score was tied, with each team correctly answering every question. This would be my question, and I was determined not to make the first mistake. Mr. Tibbets turned to me.

"What square dancing term fits this description: dancers advance and pass right shoulders. Without turning, each dancer moves to the right, passing in back of the other dancer. Then, moving backwards, each passes the other's left shoulder, returning to starting position."

I didn't spend a night with Mr. Corrigan for nothing.

"That is a do-si-do."

"Correct," Mr. Tibbets said.

I smiled to myself. That was slicker than grass through a goose.

The Garfield High School team answered the seventeenth question correctly. Therefore, it was up to Lisa to answer the eighteenth question correctly in order for our team to get a chance to answer the bonus question. If we got the bonus question right, we would tie Garfield and make it to sudden death.

"What Swiss-German psychoanalyst was instrumental in bringing psychology into the twentieth century by developing one of several theories of the unconscious, especially in formulating theories on the collective unconscious and the archetypes?"

"Carl Jung," Lisa replied without hesitation.

"Correct. Now, for the bonus question: researchers believe that this animal, the biggest, fiercest predator in the Age of the Reptiles, lacked muscle in its legs and was actually slow of foot. Can you name it?"

"I spent my entire childhood reading every dinosaur book ever written," Mike whispered. "It's the Tyrannosaurus Rex."

"Tyrannosaurus Rex," Lisa said aloud as I held my breath.

"Correct." I allowed myself to exhale and Mr. Tibbets continued, "We will now move to sudden death. I will ask questions, alternating between the two teams until one team misses and the other team answers correctly. Any team member may buzz in and answer the question."

We went back and forth three times before Mr. Tibbets asked the unthinkable.

"State the quadratic formula."

A member from the Garfield team hit her buzzer. "X equals b plus or minus the square root of b squared minus four ac, all over two a."

"That is incorrect," Mr. Tibbets said. "Can anyone from the St. Hilary's team answer this correctly?"

Tim and I both went for the buzzer at the same time, but I beat him by a millisecond. I closed my eyes.

"X equals *negative* b plus or minus the square root of b squared minus four ac, all over two a."

"Correct!" Mr. Tibbets shouted. "St. Hilary's High School is this year's Academic Quiz Bowl Champion!" The audience broke into deafening applause.

We hurdled out of our seats in celebration, jumping up and down and hugging each other in an ecstatic circle.

"They'll remember our name now," I screamed to Lisa over the noise, "because everyone remembers the name of the champion!"

Chapter
Nineteen

To celebrate our victory, my parents threw together an impromptu party for Sunday afternoon. Shortly after five p.m., Tim and his family arrived. I opened the door and Tim sauntered in whistling *We Are the Champions*. The Davises and Finnegans arrived next.

"What would you like to drink?" my dad asked Mike and Lisa. "We have cola, lemonade, water . . ."

"No more questions!" Mike exclaimed. "I'll take whatever you've got."

After Ms. Jackson arrived, my mom wanted a picture of us all with the celebratory cake.

"Everyone move in closer," my mom commanded, aiming the camera at us.

As Tim leaned against me, I could feel my heart pumping rapidly. Afraid he could feel it, I called out, "Any day now, Mom!"

"I've got it," she said, snapping the picture. "Let's do a few more—I think Mia's mouth was open in that one."

"That wouldn't be unusual," Tim commented.

"I heard that," I said, elbowing him hard in the ribs.

Finally, the pizzas were delivered and everyone spread out to eat and talk. Mike, Lisa, Tim, and I sat in a circle on the floor of the family room, reliving our glory moments from the day before, talking on top of each other.

"I could've died when Mia answered the question on the quadratic formula," Lisa said.

Mike shook his head. "How in the world she pulled that out of her head, I will never know."

"It was my expert teaching," Tim exclaimed. "It was well worth your five bucks. Wasn't it, Mia?"

"I didn't understand a word you said." I said, playfully pushing him over. "I swear, I was channeling Mr. Grizzling in my brain."

Lisa made a face. "How repugnant. Mr. Grizzling was in your brain?"

"So, were you channeling Mr. Corrigan when you answered the square dancing question?" Mike asked.

"It was my expert dancing!" Tim shouted. "I'm telling you, Mia gets all her knowledge from me."

"Would you shut up?" I said, throwing my pizza crust at him.

Ms. Jackson sat down with us. "I can't believe you knew the answers to all those questions yesterday. Even I didn't know some of them."

"Who told us we had to live, eat, and breathe trivia?" I asked.

"I didn't think you really would, Mia," Ms. Jackson said with a laugh. "My blood pressure was sky high during a few tense moments yesterday. In fact, I still need to cool down."

"That can be arranged," my mom said, getting out the ice cream containers. "I've cut the cake, but I can't seem to find the ice cream scoop. Have either of you seen it?"

I shook my head. "I haven't had ice cream all week."

"I think it's in the garage," Chris said. "There was a dead bird in the backyard, and I used it to scoop it up and throw it away."

My mom gasped. "Chris!"

"I think we have an ice cream scoop at our house you can use," Mrs. Radford offered. "Tim, will you go over and get it? Mia, could you go with him so he brings back the right thing? Usually, Tim listens to only half of what I say."

"I know how you feel, Mrs. Radford. I have to be his science partner, and he doesn't follow directions in there, either." I rose from the floor and started to follow Tim out the door.

"At least I didn't set the lab on fire," Tim replied.

"*I* set the lab on fire? It was *your* fault the table caught fire!"

"Who was stirring the test tube?"

"Who was bothering me?"

"Here we go again," Lisa moaned. "Go get the ice cream scoop and quit fighting!"

"Yeah, I'm hungry," Mike called.

"We're going—that is, if Mia would hurry up," Tim said, pushing me out the door.

"You're so slow it takes you an hour and a half to watch *Sixty Minutes*," I replied, pushing him back. I closed the door behind us. "Lisa's right. We need to stop arguing all the time. I just can't take it any more. Is there anything we can do to end our war?"

"I know one way." Tim leaned over and gently kissed me.

This time, I didn't pull away. Instead, I pulled out my retainer and kissed him back. After a long, glorious kiss, I finally stepped away.

"I like the way you call a truce," I said.

"Would you like to sign another peace treaty?" Tim asked hopefully.

"I'm all for world peace." I smiled and kissed Tim again.

We were in the middle of enjoying our peace accord, when suddenly Tim was ripped out of my arms by an enraged Jake.

"Step off!" he shouted as he punched Tim in the face. "What do you think you're doin', triflin' with my chassy?"

Tim fell to the ground and Jake jumped on top of him, pummeling him with his fists. Tim's lip split open and began spewing blood. Furiously, Tim grabbed Jake by the shirt and rolled him over. In a fit of rage, he wailed on Jake with his fists. Blood was flying everywhere.

"Jake, what are you doing here?" I said, grabbing Tim by the back of his shirt and pulling him off Jake. "Both of you, stop it!"

Tim punched Jake one last time, and then stood up, gasping for breath. Jake hoisted himself off the ground and panted.

"I had my mom drop me off here so I could give you props for your big win yesterday."

I bit my lip. "Oh, that's nice."

"That's what I thought, too." He brushed himself off. "Then I caught this punk gettin' all up in my bizzness. If he hurt you, I swear I'll cap on him."

Tim lunged for Jake again.

"Like you could," Tim said. "And besides, I didn't hurt her. She wanted me to kiss her!"

I threw myself between them.

"Tim, go to your house, clean up, and calm down. I need to talk with Jake alone."

"I don't trust him with you," Tim said, wiping the blood off his chin.

"Dude," Jake replied, spitting blood, "you're whacked. Mia and I are goin' out! I can't trust *you.*"

I stared intently into Tim's eyes and rested my hand on his arm. "Please leave us alone. I'll meet you back at my house in a little while."

Tim shrugged my hand off and grudgingly walked away. I pulled Jake over to my old swing set in the backyard.

"Are you all right? You're bleeding," I said gently, sitting down on a swing.

"That punk couldn't hurt me. But I need to know: Were you really creepin' on me, dude, or did Tim make you kiss him?" Jake grabbed my swing, forcing me to look him in the eye. I sighed.

"Jake, I'm so sorry. I didn't plan to kiss Tim—it just happened."

"But I thought we had somethin' goin' on," Jake said, wiping the blood off his face. "I really like you, dude. So, I guess if this is the only time it happened, we can still keep chillin' together."

"Well," I stammered.

"You've been creepin' on me before today?"

"Only once," I said quickly.

"But I thought you were all hot to be my breezy," Jake stammered. "It was all going so good. And I was like . . . totally understanding when you dissed me to study for that jankity Test Bowl."

"Quiz Bowl."

"Whatever."

"Jake, you and I have nothing in common." I sighed again. "I think it would be better if we didn't go out any more."

"You think I'm stupid, don't you?"

"No, it's not that—"

"'Cuz I'm not. And I was lying when I said you were bootylicious. You're just some raggedy chick who'd be nothing without me. Let's get serious. Do you really think you'd be class president if you weren't dating me? I took you from being totally whack and made you Miss Thing. And you're telling me you're baggin' me? That's a total laugh because *I'm* droppin' *you!*"

"Jake, please, I didn't mean to hurt your feelings."

"That's a joke," Jake spat. "A jankity chick like you, hurting my feelings? I was only using you to pass your betty's class. The fact you were so easy was just a bonus. In fact, I've never dated a girl who was so quick to jump my bones as you. As soon as I used you up, I was going to drop you anyway because you'll never be worthy of a slammin' guy like me."

"Is that so?" I exploded. "Well, let me tell you something, you ghetto-talking wannabe. I am not a 'chick,' 'chassy,' 'breezy,' or a 'dude.' St. Hilary's is not in the hood, and you live in a million dollar home. Face it, Jake, you're a poser! And for your information, I won the election on my own with help from my *real* friends. The only thing you were right about is that I'm so much smarter than you, it's pathetic. You even make me believe in reincarnation, because nobody could be as stupid as you in one lifetime. And by the way, when you go crawling back to Cassie, you'd better work on your kissing skills, because kissing you is like making out with a toad!"

I jumped off my swing and left Jake speechless in the backyard. I marched back into my kitchen and found my mom placing slices of cake onto plates.

"I thought I heard Jake out there. Why don't you invite him in for some cake and ice cream?"

"I don't think Jake will be coming around here any more," I said.

"Is that so?" my mom asked, raising an eyebrow. "By the way, what happened to Tim and the ice cream scoop?"

"Here it is!" Tim yelled, running through the back door.

"Oh, my goodness!" said my mom, rushing over to examine Tim's cut lip and the beginning of a black eye. "Are you all right? Mia didn't do this to you, did she?"

"Mom!" I said.

"I'm fine," Tim said. "I just had a little trouble finding the ice cream scoop."

"Gosh, I'd hate to see you if we'd sent you over for the cake knife," my mom commented, deciding Tim's injuries weren't fatal. "Why don't you two come out to the living room for some cake and ice cream?"

"Thanks, Mrs. Fullerton, but may I talk to Mia alone first?"

"Sure, but if you come back with a broken arm, I'm contacting the authorities."

I followed Tim out to the backyard and didn't see any sign of Jake. He must have started on his long walk home. I couldn't help but be a little pleased—it was so chilly outside, yet Jake thought he was too cool to wear a jacket.

Tim picked up the basketball and threw it to me. "Want to play a little one-on-one?" he said.

"Haven't you been beaten up enough today?" I smiled, dribbling the ball.

Tim took the ball from my hand and shot a free throw. "So, what did you say to Jake?"

"Let's just say that Jake and I are over," I said, rebounding the ball.

"So, where does that leave us?" Tim asked, stealing the ball from me and shooting a lay-up.

"What do *you* think?" I said, grabbing the ball.

Tim stopped and, leaning over, quickly kissed me as he stole the ball from my hands.

"I think you're going to get trounced in this basketball game," he said.

"Oh yeah? Bring it on, tough guy," I said with a grin.

Tim threw an air ball. "So, have you read the new Todd Lacey book?"

"Of course I did," I said, rebounding the ball. "It's a great commentary on how women are the backbone of society."

Tim blocked my shot. "No way. It's about how men have had to carry women along through the ages."

"You've got to be kidding! You totally missed the point of the book."

"I think you'd better reread it," Tim said, dropping the ball. "If you want, I can underline all the important points."

I scrambled after the ball and made a three-pointer. "There are only several people in this world I find obnoxious, and you are all of them."

Tim rebounded the ball. "Then why do you like me so much?"

"Because I know I can beat you in basketball," I said, stealing the ball and making a shot over his head. "Why do you like me?"

"Because I can do this," Tim said as he grabbed me from behind, twirled me around, and began to kiss me.

That night, as my roller coaster plunged downward into darkness, I held my hands up and screamed excitedly, taking pleasure in the ride. Surprisingly, my car never reached the ground. Instead, as it continued up another hill, I held on and smiled, wondering where the ride would take me next.

Acknowledgements

A special thank you to my husband Todd and my children Erin and Nolan for being incredibly supportive of me and my writing career.

Thank you to my extended family and friends for everything you do for me. I'd especially like to thank my parents Pat and Bonnie Burke for their continued belief that I can do anything I set my mind to; my siblings Joe Burke, Maureen Stager, and Michelle Juarez for their humor; Elaine Koonce for her friendship; my book club colleagues for their encouragement; Mike Abrams and Kathy Anderson for their edits; and my writing group, Jan Blazanin and Sharelle Byars Moranville, for everything.

Thank you to the Iowa Chapter of the Society of Children's Book Writers and Illustrators. I am blessed to be among such amazing talent. I would also like thank the incredible writers I read while growing up, especially Paula Danziger.

This book would not exist without the inspiration of all my former students. Thank you for supplying me enough material to last a lifetime.

Most of all, I'd like to thank Ronda Lindsay for pulling *Mia the Meek* out of the slush pile at Bancroft Press, and publisher Bruce Bortz, who agreed Mia was a character richly deserving long literary life.

A Note from the Author

Growing up in a household filled with my older brother and sister, a teen-age aunt, and a younger brother with special needs, I soon discovered that if I wanted any of my parents' attention, I'd have to be creative to get it. So, I told funny stories to make them laugh.

My love of story-telling grew as I entered the wonderful world of reading, and I spent much of my childhood curled up with a good book in front of a heat register in my family's living room in Davenport, Iowa. Sometimes, I'd become so engrossed in a book, I wouldn't even notice the heat vent burning my arm! But until the seventh grade, I hadn't connected the joy of reading with the joy of writing stories. That's when my English teacher, Mrs. Hermie, signed me up to attend a writer's workshop for talented writers. Just by having someone tell me I could write led to a burst of creativity during my junior high years.

My love of writing continued, and when I became a middle school language arts teacher, I often found myself writing side-by-side with my students. One day, after listening to my students grumble when I assigned them the task of writing a realistic book of fiction, I told them I would share their pain and attempt to write one, too.

And that is when Mia Fullerton was born. Even after my students' books were graded and returned to them, I couldn't stop writing about Mia and her friends. I combined many of my own embarrassing moments—yes, I actually set my lab table on fire during my freshman year at Assumption Catholic high school—with my students' anecdotes to create the fictional world of St. Hilary's, and I haven't stopped writing since.

Unfortunately, a person needs more than a passion for writing in order to get published. So, I sadly said good-bye to my classroom and focused on learning the craft of writing instead. After many years, many revisions, and many rejection letters, Mia finally found a home at Bancroft Press, and I have been given the gift of being able to re-visit Mia and her friends as I begin writing this book's sequel, *Mia the Melodramatic*.

I currently live in Urbandale, Iowa with my husband, Todd, two children (Erin and Nolan), and my very ornery dog, Casey.

About the Author

Born and educated in Iowa, Eileen Boggess earned both her bachelor's and master's degrees in education from the University of Northern Iowa in Cedar Falls, IA. As an undergraduate, she minored in English and Language Arts.

Her first job after college was as a teacher for St. John/St. Nicholas Catholic School in Waterloo, Iowa, where she taught a combined class of fifth and sixth graders. She later moved to Urbandale, IA, where she taught middle school language arts and gifted education for St. Pius X School. While there, she coached Mock Trial, Future Problem Solvers, Destination Imagination, and speech and debate, and started a quarterly newspaper written and designed by students.

In 2002, she branched out as a freelance writer, covering, among other things, education and business for the *Press Citizen* newspaper. In 2003, she won a writing contest sponsored by *Writer's Digest Magazine*.

She is an adjunct faculty member for Upper Iowa University and currently teaches a children's literature course. She also supervises student teachers for the university.

She is a member of the Society of Children's Book Writers & Illustrators and an enthusiastic participant in the Iowa chapter's activities.

Mia the Meek is her first published book.